Love is Blind

N.OWENS

LOVE IS BLIND

Copyright 2024 by N. OWENS, USA

All rights reserved.

This is a work of fiction. Names, characters, places, and incidents portrayed in this novel are products of the author's imagination or are used fictitiously. Any resemblance to actual individuals, living or otherwise, events or locations is entirely coincidental.

No part of this publication may be reproduced, stored in a retrieval system, or transmitted in any form or by any means, electronic, mechanical, photocopying, recording, or otherwise. This is done without prior permission of the copyright owner, except as permitted by US copyright law.

Dedication

This one is for the ones who lived through all the toxic relationships and finally found your prince charming.

I've lived through it and found mine.

So, here's to you all finding yours!

Trigger Warning

Please read possible triggers before continuing. Your mental health is important to me.
This is a dark romance book containing some dark themes.
This is a why choose romance, meaning the FMC ends up with more than one love interest.
Sexual Interactions, Past trauma, Possessive MMC, Adult Content, Mention of Domestic Violence, Unaliving and more.
If you have any questions or concerns, please reach out and contact N.Owens at Nowensauthor@hotmail.com

Prologue - Xander

"We will give him 10 minutes tops tonight. It's not our fault that he was late for the meeting that he wanted and that we had to leave. Tonight is about Wren, and I don't want her anywhere near this side of business. So, he gets 10 minutes, then we tell him to fuck off and to leave us alone." I hiss, annoyed at the fact we even have to entertain the idea of meeting with Adrian tonight. We all agreed, his business aspirations don't align with ours. He is too power hungry ever since his father passed.

A soft clearing of a throat has me turning to the hallway. "I present to you, your perfect woman." From the corner of my eye, I saw the small, dark-haired woman who was helping Wren get ready to give a little bow, but I kept my eyes on the beautiful blonde bombshell in front of me.

Jaxon on my right hitches a breath. All three of our jaws hit the ground as we take in Wren. "Guys, this is where you comment on your woman and how beautiful she looks." The dark hair girl snaps, crossing her arms on her chest, expectedly. Wren's lips turn down in a frown before rushing out words.

"She didn't mean it like that. You don't have t-" I step forward and place my finger to her lips to quiet her.

"Oh, Little bird. Your friend is right. You are breathtaking and that's what you did. The moment we saw you standing there, we lost all words. You are a goddess among us mortals." I lean down, lifting her chin as I go, before kissing her plumb soft lips.

"Can we say swoon worthy?" Abby whispers from the side of me, making me and the guys chuckle.

"Guys, this is my new personal assistant, Abby. Jax said she can work for me. And that she can live here." Wren informs me, nibbling on her lip nervously.

"Princess, I filled them in. They understand what is going on. We have already run a background check on her as well. She may move in whenever she is ready." Wren's face lights up at Jax's words. "Marie will sort everything out for you, Abby."

"Thank you. I will assist with whatever anyone needs. I make a mean coffee, by the way." We chuckle again. "You all better get going. Make sure she eats as well; she's only had a snack while I was getting her ready." She makes the shooing motion as I slide my hand down around Wren's lower back and shift to lead her towards the front door.

"I think you and her together might be trouble." I whisper before nipping at her ear. "But you really do look absolutely stunning tonight, Wren." She looks beyond stunning in her silver-gray long-sleeved dress. It forms to her perfect body, flaring out at her hips with a long slit that exposes her creamy thighs. The corset area is a delicate floral lace that leads up to her chest and pushes up her breast to tease a saint into sinning.

As we hit the open door, goosebumps pebble across her skin. We head down a few steps and Mav opens the back door, reaching out to help Wren into the backseat.

"Angel, you look delicious and just like the nickname I gave you." He skims his nose up her neck and I hear a faint moan cross her lips. "You smell so good, too." He adds on a big inhale, making her give a full-body shiver.

"Mav. Behave." Jax snaps, making Mav finally lean away. Jax leans in and takes the seat across to her as Mav claims her other side. "Princess, you look beautiful. Are you ready for tonight?"

"Yes, nervous but excited, I guess." Her already rosy cheeks blush even more. Wren finally relaxes back into the seat as we all chat about useless things. After a few minutes of driving, I place my hand on her thigh, feeling the warmth of her body seep into me. It doesn't take long until we are pulling up to the gala entrance.

"Wren, I need you to listen to me." I turn to face her. "You do not leave our sides. You need to go to the bathroom? One of us will go with you. Wanna take a walk? One of us will go with you. Do you understand?" She nods before answering me with a "yes." My tone is firm, knowing that tonight everyone will see her with us, and it will be a clear statement to some.

Jax must see something on her face because he continues. "Wren breathe. Nothing will happen to you. You're safe with us. We will keep you safe, Princess. Do you trust us?" He asks, and we all wait with bated breath for her answer.

"Yes." She tells him, and it's like all our shoulders drop in relief. "Good girl. Now head up, shoulders back, Princess. You are royalty." Wren takes a deep breath, lifts her head a bit higher and smiles. We all step out, one by one, and placing Wren between us all. Camera's blinding us with flashes as we nod and head for the entrance.

The room's warmth washes over us, and we've barely made it a few feet in when a familiar, excited voice calls out Wren's name. "Wren, sweetheart, you made it." Mrs.

Williams embraces Wren in a tight hug before pulling back and giving us all bright smiles. "It's been forever since the kids have seen you. They ask about you every day. When are you coming back, dear?" Wren's face lights up at the mention of Mrs. Williams' kids.

"Oh, ummm, I should be back on Monday." Her reply is hesitant, but we did promise she could go back to work soon. Whether or not we like it.

"That's great news. I will let the kids know and we will stop by. How does that sound?" Wren nods, her face still smiling with happiness. "Great, well, I have to go greet more guests, but enjoy the gala, sweetheart. If you need anything, just come find me." Before Wren or any of us can respond, Mrs. Williams is off greeting the next couple making their entrance.

"Let's go find our table and get you something to eat, Angel." Mav wraps his arm under and around Wren's and leads her over to a table with our name on it. He has her take a seat, right as someone approaches. We make it to the table just as Mav orders us all the special before handing Wren a drink. "Here, Angel, some champagne."

"Oh, thank you." She takes a sip. As we all settle in to wait for our food, the melodic strains of music fill the air, emanating from a live band playing softly in the corner. Wren begins to sway back and forth in her seat, her movement almost hypnotic, as we all just stare. It's not long before plates are being placed in front of us. The smell teasing our noses as I hear Wren's stomach let out a soft growl. She wastes no time picking up her fork and digging in, and we follow suit. We eat in silence, getting lost in the flavors of creamy pasta and crispy garlic bread. No one bothers to approach us the entire time we sit, but we keep our eyes on the room all the same.

After we eat, I suggest we make a round. I would rather get this meeting with Adrian over with sooner than later, but I haven't spotted him since we arrived. With my arm securely wrapped around Wren, I lead us around the room, feeling her warmth against my side. Mav is on her other side and Jax follows up the rear. The same position as we entered, with Wren protected at our center. We say our greetings to a few gentlemen we do legit business with, while a few ladies compliment Wren's attire before we decide to stop at a bar for a drink. Wren declines one, confirming what we already knew about her not being a big drinker.

"Good evening gentlemen, fancy seeing you here." The she devil's voice sounds from behind us, and I grind my teeth in annoyance. She must've grown a pair, knowing we can't do anything to her here with so many witnesses.

"Tiffany." I growl. "I thought we told you to get out of town. Was butchering your hair not enough of a warning?" The threat in my voice is clear, and I feel Wren tense next to me. I wrap my arm around her waist tighter and tuck her in closer to my side. "Are you that much of a psycho that you would show up here and make a scene?" I feel the other two guys press in closer to Wren, protectively as well. Especially after we witnessed what this bitch did to our woman. I give her a wicked smirk as I take in my newest handy work. It's obvious she went and had someone try to help her fix the rat's nest, but it still screams choppy and cheap.

She lifts her head, narrowing her eyes on where I hold Wren to me, and scoffs. "Not everything is about you, Xander. I'm actually here with my boyfriend." She pauses, looking behind us, and smiles. "Oh, there he is, baby, over here." She calls out in a high-pitched whine.

Mav snorts. "Figures. She jumps from dick to dick like it's some type of competition. What dumbass was stupid enough to fall for her bullshit this time?" He asks, but no one answers as we wait to see which dumbass did, in fact, fall for her bullshit.

We tense as Adrian West comes over to stand next to Tiffany, wrapping his arm around her to make it clear they are together. "Baby, these are the guys I was telling you about." Everyone stays quiet as we stare at each other.

Adrian's eyes flash to Wren before doing a double take. His lips turning down in a frown as he stares at our woman. I'm about to tell him he is close to losing his eyes when he speaks. "Dolly?" He questions in a confused tone, but Wren's reaction tells me everything I need to know already.

In a flash, Wren's body goes limp in my arms. Jax and Mav rushing to help cover her dead weight. "Wren? Wren baby. Can you hear me?" No response. I turn to demand answers, but Adrian is already dragging Tiffany towards the doors, and we don't have time to go after him. Wren needs us.

"I think she fainted. Let's get her home." Jax says as I bend and lift Wren up into my arms. Mrs. Williams spots me first, a shocked look on her face, and rushes over.

"Oh dear, what happened?" Her eyes shift to each of us, slightly accusing, but I don't take offense. I understand why. There are tons of rumors about us, good and horrible, but we would never hurt Wren.

"We're not sure. She fainted a minute ago. We are going to get her home and have a doctor come check her out. Thank you for inviting us. I'll have Wren give you a call when she is feeling better." Mav explains and after a long hesitant look, Mrs. Williams nods, and we are heading out the doors.

Our car is pulling up, and I turn to Jax and Mav. "I want everything you can find on Adrian and if Wren has any connection to him. A reaction like this is too extreme to not be connected somehow. Get everyone we know on it."

In the next minute, both guys are making calls and sending texts as we climb into the back of the limo, Wren still cradled in my lap. I think back to what Adrian called Wren and frown. He called her Dolly. Why? What is she hiding from us, and how did we not find anything sooner? As we get closer to home, I send a quick text to have Doc stop by in the morning to make sure everything is okay with her. Considering the long night ahead of us, we'll give her a chance to rest for the time being. Because only one thing is playing in my mind.

Adrian West is now a dead man.

Chapter One

Wren

The remnants of my living nightmare cling to me as I break free and slowly wake. I'm covered in sticky sweat and my heart is pounding faster than a racehorse on a track. Staying as still as possible, I take in my surroundings. I don't believe the guys would let that monster take me, but you can never be too sure who you can really trust.

Taking stock of my body, I realize I'm no longer in the silky soft dress I wore to the gala. This fabric feels soft still, more like a t-shirt, and my legs are bare but for a pair of fuzzy feeling socks. I'm not in any pain, and if Adrian got a hold of me, that's exactly what I would be feeling.

My mind is still foggy, but I remember we were taking a walk around the room and stopped to get a quick drink. Then Tiffany showed up and called over her supposed new boyfriend. That's when someone else came around and even with no eyesight, I could feel the evil coming from him, but then he spoke one word. Dolly. That stupid fucking name he would call me. That voice is unmistakable. I could pick it out from a crowd without hesitation. It's the leading role in all my nightmares. It all came rushing back then, our meeting, thinking I was in love for the first time. I thought he was my forever, the perfect man, until it all changed.

It started with small things like him ordering things for me. Then the side remarks about how I need to watch my figure and that I wouldn't be young and beautiful forever. He would order me clothes that weren't my style and a size or two too small. He would say they were gifts, that he wanted me to have nice, pretty things. Of course, I listened to everything he said because we were in love. He just wanted to show me he loved me and I wanted to make him happy. I wasn't allowed to hang out with my friends. It was expected of me to comply with all his choices for my attire and follow his instructions on what and when I could eat. I knew something was wrong, and I should have run the first time he hit me, but once again, I was in love.

Amber, my best friend, told me something wasn't right with him. She said the way he looked at me wasn't right, that it was like he wanted to own me, like a pet, and not like he loved me. I suppose I was his pet or toy dolly as he started calling me.

It was always my fault for the beatings or the "lessons," as he called them. I needed to learn to behave and be a proper lady. He wanted me to be the perfect little submissive girlfriend and, if I could be that, the pain would stop. Some nights, he would show me off to his friends and business partners, showing them how well he trained me. It was humiliating, but what else could I do? Everything of mine was now controlled by him. My bank account, all my money I had saved before he made me quit my job. He told me he would take care of me, but only if he could trust me. My trust came at the price of signing my life away, but at the time I was madly in love and would do anything for Adrian.

We met at college. I was taking business classes because my dream was to own a bookshop. Amber took the same classes because we were going to open up a shop together. I never paid attention to anyone else in the class until one day Amber missed class because she was sick. The chair was pulled out next to me and there he was, Adrian West, with all his boys' next door glory. He was every girl's dream guy, sweet, charming, and incredibly handsome. He had blonde hair, blue eyes and a smooth voice and I fell head over heels fast. Once class was over, he invited me to coffee, and from that point forward, wherever he was, I was. Amber warned me then too, but I wouldn't listen. I thought maybe she was jealous that I met someone, but I wish I had listened to her.

Looking back, I think he chose me that day. I was quiet and kept to myself, except for Amber, and when he gave me attention, I became hooked like a little needy puppy. An easy target. What a young, naïve fool I was.

Lost in my thoughts of the past, I feel the bed shift next to me, causing me to flinch automatically. I hear a curse, which only causes me to jerk away from the person again. "Princess, you're okay. You're safe." Jax?

"Jaxon, give her some space." The stern voice of Xander fills the room next. The bed shifts again, as I'm guessing Jax gets up. I take a deep, calming breath before sitting up and turning to where I heard the guys speak.

"Ummm... what happened?" I remember hearing Adrian, then feeling fear and the urge to run and hide, but then nothing. How did I get here? And what will happen now that Adrian knows I'm alive?

"What do you remember from last night, Angel?" Mav asks somewhere to my right. His voice sounds strange, his usually low tone is still there, but I swear I almost hear worry.

I debated for a second what to tell these men. I think they know something bad happened to me, but they could never understand how bad it truly was. Plus, I doubt they really care all that much. Yes, they say they want me, but I doubt they would want me if they knew what I've been through. I'm weak and if I could still see, I'm pretty sure I would be afraid of my own shadow. "Well, we went to the gala, had dinner, then we walked around the room so you guys could mingle." I tilt my head to the side, making it seem like I'm trying to recall, but really I'm thinking about how to explain the next part. "We stopped to get drinks when that woman, Tiffany, showed up. She called over her new boyfriend and then nothing." I lie. I know who showed up, but they can't know how I know him. That part of my life died when that bastard left me to die on the side of the road.

"That's all you remember?" Xander asks, but there is a tone to his questions that screams he doesn't believe me. I nod.

"Yeah, did I pass out or something? I wasn't feeling too well yesterday morning, either." I lie again. Staring straight ahead, I wait for one of them to reply. After what feels like hours, Xander speaks again.

"Little bird?" The way he says my nickname has me furrowing my brow and focusing my attention on him as I look up towards where I heard his voice. He is standing in front of me, I know that, but since I'm still seated on the bed, he sounds taller. "Who's Dolly?" My back straightens at the nickname coming from his mouth as my blood runs cold again. How can a five-letter word have such an effect on me?

"I- I... I have no idea. W-Why?" I say, but even I can hear the shaky fear in my response.

"Don't lie to us, Wren. Who is Adrian West to you, and why did he call you Dolly?" Xander demands, and the cold, demanding tone causes chills to run up my back. This is the man I remember hearing that night in the alley months ago. He shot a man like it was nothing for beating on a woman, but what would he do if he knew what I lived through? What Adrian West put me through?

When I say nothing, I feel the bed dip next to me before huge, rough hands grasp me. "Princess. The moment Adrian saw you, there was recognition all over his face. When he called you Dolly, you freaked out before you fainted. It's obvious to us he knows you and you know him. You made it clear with your body language that he scares you. Now he's in the wind, and we can't find him to ask him why. So, tell us what happened, and we can figure out the next step." Jax's thumb runs across my skin in soothing swipes, and it's almost enough to make me spill it all. But the words just won't come.

"Angel, why don't we take a shower, get you cleaned up? All we did was change you last night. Abby wanted to get you cleaned up, but we figured you needed some rest, but now you look like a raccoon." I hear a slap and Mav grunt. "What it's true? She looks like a sexy raccoon." I let out a giggle, assuming I probably look like a mess after last night. Who knew my grumpy, easily annoyed Maverick would be the one to know I just needed a little something to distract me and give me time to build my shields up a bit?

"Yes, please. That actually sounds nice right now." I send a smile in the direction I heard his voice.

"Fine, but after a shower and some food, we want an explanation, Wren." I gulp, the nerves that started to ease coming back tenfold.

I haven't told a single soul about what happened that night. Amber only knows because she is the one who found me. She saw the evidence and nursed me back to health before disappearing with me. She doesn't know why he did it, just that it was him and I wanted that night buried away forever, but that can't happen now. I'm falling for these men, and I don't think I can pretend I'm fine anymore. But I fear what will happen now, what Adrian will do. What if he tries to hurt my men? My men? That thought causes an internal reaction I've only ever felt for Amber. Protectiveness. Right then and there, I knew I had to tell them the truth and everything that happened. They need to know that Adrian West could be a threat to them.

"Okay. You're right." I take a deep breath, steeling my spine at my decision to tell the truth to these men. "You have a right to know." Jax's hand tightens around mine, giving me a bit of his strength. "I'll tell you everything, but you will not like it." I say, but I have a feeling they already know that.

"Okay, well, come on, Angel. I'll scrub your back for you." Another giggle slips free as Mav grabs my other hand to help me off the bed and leads me to the bathroom.

Looking back on the last month of being here with them, I realize they are completely different men around me than when I overhear them working. Maybe we could make this work, and I'll get my own kind of twisted fairy-tale ending. A girl can dream.

Chapter Two

Wren

It's like the hot water just washes away the stress of the last hour, the moment I step under the spray. My shoulders relax as I just soak up the heat and steam. I feel Mav step in behind me, and I step aside so he can wash up, too. Feeling around, I try to find my shampoo, but right as my fingers reach for the hard plastic of the bottle, it disappears. "I said I would help you, Angel. Let me take care of you." I don't bother with a response, since I've learned it doesn't matter what I say. These guys will do what they want, so I give him a nod of my head. "Good girl. Now turn around." His hands grip my hips and slowly turn me so that my back is now facing him. "Lean your head back." I do as he says and feel the cool gel touch my scalp a second behind Maverick's fingers, gently rubbing it all in. His fingers do their magic and a small, satisfied moan escapes my throat before I can stop it.

"Does that feel good?" He asks and this time I nod because I don't think I could even use my words if I wanted. "Good, now let's wash it out." He pulls me back against his firm soap chest and then pulls me back under the spray of water. I shut my eyes, blocking out the world as he rinses away the soapy residue. Soon after, his body presses against mine, urging me to move forward. I feel his hard length nestle between my cheeks, and I try to ignore the needy whimper building. I must not have hidden it very well because Mav's hot breath is against my ear as his hand glides across my stomach and down between my thighs.

"Do you need something, Angel? Are you feeling needy for me?" he purrs, the sound going straight to my pussy.

It takes a long second to breathe through my need, but I finally find the words. "Y-Yes. I need you." And I do. I need something to help me process that I'm about to tell someone my deep, dark secrets and relive a nightmare I've been trying to forget. Mav can make me feel something, even if it's just for a moment. I need to feel alive, to remember I made it out and have been free for years. I'm stronger than in my past.

Maverick's finger skates across my skin as his dick twitches behind me. The asshole stops right before reaching my center. "Ask nicely." His voice is thick with lust as he thrusts his hips against me, grinding his hard on against my ass.

"P-please Maverick." He lets out a groan as his fingers finally dip lower and pinch my nub, causing me to jump a bit. Letting out a deep chuckle, his fingers dive lower until he is teasing my opening.

"I love it when you say my name." Shoving his finger into my core, I'm instantly moaning out at the feeling of being filled by this man. "Now, just let me take care of you, Angel." I slump back against his chest and let him fuck me with his fingers. In and out, in and out, he keeps a steady pace, and I must've been needing this more than I thought because I'm reaching a climax in minutes. My pussy flutters around his fingers, my back arches as a wave of bliss builds, but right as I'm about to crash over the wave into pure euphoria, Mav yanks away his fingers. I cry out in protest as my pussy tries to tighten around nothing now.

"Oh no, baby, if you're going to come, it's going to be on my cock." Then he flips me around, hands gripping my hips, and then I'm lifted. The sudden change in position has my head spinning, the breath leaving my lungs in a gasp, and I immediately reach out and wrap my legs and arms around Mav. "Hold on, baby." I feel him lean back, and then I feel him reach between us. Knowing what he is doing, I lean back a bit to give him better access. He lines himself up, his tip barely tickling my entrance. "Hang tight Angel. I'm going to fuck you till you see stars." Before I can respond, Mav is slamming home and doing just as he promised.

Maverick wastes no time fucking me senseless, and I'm cumming in record time. He gives me at least two orgasms before he finally starts to chase his own high. His hands are gripping my ass so tight as he slams into me. I'm pretty sure I'll have fingertip bruises on my ass tomorrow. Not that I'm complaining. His pace gets faster, harder, and I know he's close. "Fuck. Wren, your pussy feels so fucking good." Slam, slam, slam. "Shit. Fuck. Baby, I'm about to cum. Cum with me, baby." He leans forward and his mouth wraps around my nipple and a second later, he bites down. The pinch of pain causes my body to tumble into one last climax as my pussy tightens around Mav's shaft, milking him of his juices. He groans out, the sound long and low as his pace slows. We stay like that for another few minutes until we can catch our breath.

I loosen my legs around his hips, and he helps me slide down his body. Good thing we were in the shower because I feel a mess again. Without another word, Mav continues to wash my hair and body. We stay quiet as he switches to cleaning himself, just at peace with each other at that moment. The water shuts off, and I hear the door slide open. Reaching forward, I feel for Mav. I step into his space and feel for his chest before hugging him. "Thank you, Mav. Somehow, you knew I needed this?" His arms wrap around me tight, but he says nothing, and I don't need him too.

I feel a towel wrap around me from behind. "Alright, you two, Xander is downstairs with food. Let's not keep him waiting." Jax says as he lifts me up and shifts me away from Mav. Jax mumbles something sounding like "lucky bastard" under his breath. But I can't be sure because reality comes crashing back, ruining my peace. I now have to explain a part of my past that literally gives me nightmares.

"Princess. Everything will be okay. I promise." Jax kisses the top of my head as he leads me back into the room to dress. I'm on autopilot as I dress in one of the guy's t-shirts and a pair of leggings. Jax made me put on another pair of fuzzy socks and I appreciate it now as the guys lead me downstairs and to the kitchen. The smell of food wraps around, and my stomach lets out a loud grumble. One of the guy's chuckle, before I'm being sat in a chair, a fork shoved into my hand and food being placed in front of me.

"Eat." Xander says, and I sigh, deciding to just do what he wants right now. The longer I can stall, the more I can prepare. At least, I hope so. We all eat in silence, and I can only tell they are eating as well by the noises they make. My mind wanders to where I should start story time at, from the very beginning or from where it got bad. Or the reason he might have been so shocked to see me.

I finish entirely too soon and sit there, nerves rushing through my body as I fumble with the edge of the t-shirt. It smells like Xander, the whiskey and natural manly scent fill my nose the longer I sit and stall. Someone clears their throat, making me jump and snapping my head up in that direction.

"Let's all move to the den. Wren, would you like a drink?" Xander's tone is softer than before, and I think he realizes how much just the thought of explaining all this is affecting me.

I take a deep breath before pushing away from the table. "Yes. I think that's a good idea. I think you all should have one as well. This isn't a pretty story." With that, I turn and head toward the den, hands outstretched toward any furnishings or walls.

Here goes nothing.

Chapter Three

Wren

It's "date night," which really means Adrian wants to go out and show off his pretty little trained doll. I sit at the vanity wrapped in a robe, adding the finishing touches to my hair and makeup. I was never a fan of painting my face with chemicals, but it's now expected of me. Plus, it helps hide the tired bags under my eyes and the occasional bruise on my face when Adrian forgets his temper. The man learned that people might ask questions if they see the evidence he leaves, so now he focuses more on parts of my body that can hide the marks with clothes.

I just finished my last curl when the man of the hour waltz's in like he owns the world. He doesn't. As far as I've seen, his father owns everything and Adrian is just biding his time until it's all handed over to him. I know little *about what he and his father do, but I've overheard a few whispers, and none of them sound good. I've heard they do deals with some type of cartel, having to do with drugs and guns. Rumors of shady business deals and dirty money, but I try to avoid it all. I'm simply biding my time until Adrian finds a new shiny toy to play with. I don't wish this fate on anybody, but I know I'm not Adrian's only woman. Just his main doll. I've caught the cheating asshole in the middle of the act. A woman spread out on his desk, and he had no shame. Later that night, I got the beating for interrupting his "private meeting."*

"You ready Dolly." Looking up from the table, I spot Adrian standing at the end of our bed, adjusting his cuff links. I paste on a bright, everything's perfect smile and stand.

"Yes, just need to dress." He glances down at the bed, where the dress lays in thought, and I hold my breath, hoping he doesn't change his mind and blame me for his choice. It wouldn't be the first time he changed his mind, then punish me for his wasted time. He picked out this outfit, an extremely short black mini dress, with thin straps that wrap over my shoulders and crisscross across my back. It's simple and still covers up all my lady bits, so I'm thankful.

"Well, hurry and wear those red strappy heels I like," He says, before turning and heading back out the door, calling

out over his shoulder. "You have 5 minutes. Meet me by the front door." Once his dark figure fully leaves my eyesight, the breath I was holding whooshes out of me and I almost slump back down in my chair. It's getting harder and harder to maintain my composure again around him, lately, and I think I'm hitting my breaking point.

After sucking in a full, deep lungful of air, trying to calm my erratic heart, I remember I'm on a time crunch and rush to the dress. Removing my robe, I keep my back to the large mirror in the corner, not wanting to see the proof of all my previous "lessons" with Adrian. I slip the dress on over my head and slide it down my body. I have to tug a bit to get it over my chest and hips, but once I get it on, I know it's not going anywhere. It's a snug fit, just the way he likes it. I make my way to the closet and grab the red heels he mentioned earlier, and make my way downstairs. Once I hit the bottom step, I quickly place the shoes on, before steeling my spine and praying this is one of his good nights.

Adrian is standing by the door when I approach, thumbs gliding across his phone screen. For half a second, the glow from his phone reminds me of the first time I went out with Adrian. He was a gentleman then, sweet and charming. Nothing like the monster he is now. Knowing not to interrupt him, I step up next to him and keep my head down, but from the corner of my eye I see a part of his text conversa-

tion. GET IT DONE, OR I'LL FIND SOMEONE WHO WILL. My mind races with what that could all mean, but before I can get lost in my thoughts, Adrian is tucking his phone away and glancing in my direction. He gives my body a once over before giving me a nod. I beam at his approval, but whether it's for the fact he approves of my look or that I know I won't get punished over my appearance, I will never know.

"*You look sexy, baby. Now let's get going. I have a few... friends to meet up with at the club.*" *He says friend in an odd tone, like he doesn't actually think they are friends, but I keep my mouth shut and simply smile. Grin and bear it right.*

The car ride over to the club his family owns is quiet as I watch the city fly by. My mind drifts a bit to what life would have been like for me if I hadn't met Adrian West. Would I have met some other asshole and ended up in the same situation?

I want to imagine I would have finished school and opened a bookshop with Amber by now. We would be roommates, eating ramen noodles and binge-watching old TV shows together. We would have each met a nice guy, gone out on double dates and one day get married and have kids together. But that's all-wishful hoping and dreaming.

Once we get to the club, Adrian leads us straight to his VIP booth further back in the club. The moment we sit, two half - naked servers step up, both eye fucking Adrian and asking if they can get him anything. Neither one even acknowledges me, and all Adrian says is, "I'll take my usual and a vodka soda for her." Then the asshole winks at them, like his so-called girlfriend isn't standing right next to him. Not that I care anymore what he does, but it's just another invisible slap to the face and my dignity.

Trying to make the most of my night, I decide to stand at the edge of the booth and peer over the railing. The club is actually super nice, with two enormous bars along either side of the large room. There is a DJ booth on the second floor, but the public doesn't have access to that area. There is a row of five VIP booths against the far back wall of the room where we are. Each one is a round booth with sheer fabric that circles around each to give them a sense of privacy. Adrian always sits in the one in the center, as if he is the king and needs to be the center of attention. The entire place is decorated in silver and deep navy-blue colors, with flashing neon blue and white lights overhead.

The servers return with our drinks, and before they leave, one bends down in front of my boyfriend. Her fake breast practically shoved in his face, whispers something in his ear. He gives her a smirk before smacking her ass and sending her away. Then he turns in my direction, smirk still in place, and cock a brow in question. Challenging me to say something, but he knows I won't. I've learned over the last year, the more I keep my mouth shut, the better. When he sees I'm going to keep my mouth shut, he crooks a finger, calling me over. I obey, taking a seat next to him and holding back the flinch when his hand grips my bare thigh.

He leans in and speaks into my ear. "Here, drink this." Handing me the drink he ordered, I take a small sip. I wouldn't put it past Adrian to drug me into compliance again. "We have a few minutes before the men I'm supposed to meet get here. When they do, I need you to be a good girl and continue to keep your mouth shut. Got it." Once he finishes threatening me, he leans back and gets comfortable, pulling out his phone and reading through whatever he does.

I continue to sip away at my vodka and soda, watching as the horde of people dance their night away. How incredible would it be to experience that sensation again, to lose yourself in the pulsating rhythm of the music in the middle of the dance floor? To not be anything more than someone's arm candy.

I'm lost in my daydream when a sudden pinch of pain causes me to yelp. Attempting to spin out of Adrian's hold, my efforts only intensify the pain as he tightens his grip on my hair. "I said, are you fucking listening, bitch?" He sneers at me, and I give him a small nod, letting him know I'm paying attention now. I didn't even know he was talking to me before because it's so loud in here. "Good. My new friends are here, so it's time to be a good girl, or we will need to have a lesson in behavior around my friends. Understand?"

"Y-yes Adrian." *He grins at me before giving me another rough yank, then releasing his grip.*

"Go get yourself cleaned up." *He nods to the bathroom, and I waste no time stumbling up and rushing away. Tears burn the edges of my eyes, but I refuse to let them fall. He will know he got to me, then make me pay somehow for ruining my makeup and embarrassing him. Lucky for me, the bathroom is empty, and I take a moment to lock myself in a stall.*

"You're a survivor, Wren. Grin and bear it, bide your time." *I tell myself, taking a few deep breaths to calm myself.* "He can't control you forever." *Once I'm calm enough, I straighten my dress and pull my shoulders back. I just need to sit there and look pretty. Play the perfect little doll and get through this night.*

Stepping up to the mirror, I fix a small smudge of liner, wash my hands quickly and do one more check in the mirror before pulling up my metaphorical big girl panties and heading back to the booth. I keep my head up the entire walk back, but before I get to the booth, I see Adrian and another man heading towards the back alley. Deciding he usually always wants his eyes on me, I turn and head in that direction. As I hit the back hall, the emergency exit door is closing, so I head that way, searching for Adrian. Pushing open the door, I pause, listening in case I followed the wrong direction. When I hear nothing. I step out and look in both directions, first to the right, nothing but the next street over and a couple of trash cans. Turning to my left, I freeze. I'm so shocked by what I'm seeing. The door I was holding open slips from my hand and slams shut. Adrian and another man snap their heads in my direction. Adrian has a gun to the second man's head, who is kneeling on the ground, looking beyond pissed.

The man snaps out of it first and throws a punch up and into Adrian's stomach. Adrian's gun goes off, the sound echoing off the brick walls. I'm still frozen as I watch in horror as the man grunts in pain, hands flying to his stomach. He stumbles back before tripping over his feet and falling against the wall. "T-they are going to k-kill you when they f-find o-out what you d-did." He rasps out before slumping back, eyes rolling. Adrian lets out a slew of curses, looking like a raging bull.

My mind is telling me to run, run fast and run far, but my feet won't move. Then, faster than I could have imagined, Adrian is flying towards me. His fist lands across my cheek, and my head snaps to the side, pain instantly radiating through my face. "You stupid fucking bitch. Do you have any idea what you just fucking ruined?" This time, he slaps the other side of my face. The force causes me to stumble back and fall on my ass as tears race down my cheeks.

"I-I-I..." I don't even know what to say. I just witnessed a murder. Adrian just killed a man in front of me. Oh god, he is going to kill me next. As the harsh reality dawns on me, I scramble backwards, only to have my movements halted when Adrian notices me. A second later, he delivers a forceful kick to my stomach. I curl in on myself. How did my life come to this? I knew he was abusive and honestly a piece of shit asshole but murder.

Through my tear-streaked face, I see Adrian pull out his phone and make a call. "Bring the car around to the back alley. We have a problem." Leaning down, he grips my hair and I wrap my hands around his wrist to stop him from ripping anything out as he stands and starts to drag me towards the alley entrance. "Dolly, you really fucked shit up tonight. It took me forever to set up this meeting, and you had to go and get nosey. All you fucking had to do was sit pretty and keep your mouth fucking shut. You couldn't even do that, you stupid fucking bitch." He yanks harder, making me cry out louder. I hear a car pull up in front of us and panic threatens to suffocate me. Fight, I need to fight. I kick, hit, and scream now, but I'm no match. "Shut up, you fucking bitch."

The sound of a truck door popping opening has Adrian pulling to a stop. He pulls me up by my hair until I'm kneeling on my knees, like the man was moments ago. He grins down at me. But it's not a pretty one, no. This one is full of feral rage, and it's all aimed at me. "You're going to pay for what you did tonight. Honestly, you had this a long time coming. I'm going to break you tonight, just like the dolly you are." Then he slams the butt of his gun to the top of my head and I black out.

Chapter Four

Jaxon

I watch as Wren falls apart, telling us what Adrian West did to her. Knowing there's more for her to tell, all I can do is hold her to me and reassure her she is strong. I eye Xander and Mav across the room. Mav was sitting next to her at first, but his anger was getting the best of him and needed another drink. Xander, though, I can see the rage pouring off him in waves. Everyone always assumes I'm the evil bastard of us, but Xander is usually the mastermind behind it all. I just enjoy the dirty work.

Right after Wren mentioned Adrian killing a man in an alleyway, Xander was typing away on his phone. He had a cousin who went missing a couple of years back. Oliver was a good kid and told us he was going out to a party with a few friends. We thought nothing of it since we tried to keep him out of our more unsavory business, but when we hadn't heard from him after a day or two, we sent men looking. They could never find information on what could have happened. It was like he just upped and disappeared.

"Take your time, Wren." I tell her, rubbing my hand up and down her back. It infuriates me to see her in this state, so sad and broken looking. I'm sure the guys are thinking the same thing, but when I get my hands on Adrian, I plan to show him what actual pain is. I'll prolong his survival for weeks, carefully nursing him back to health, solely to inflict further pain upon him.

"No, it's fine. I just want to get this all out. It's time for me to move on. I don't want to be afraid anymore." She lifts her head and takes a deep breath. God, she is so strong and doesn't even know it. I reach forward and swipe a bit of hair behind her ear.

"You never have to be afraid again, baby." Leaning forward, I kiss her forward and watch as her lips tilt up in a barely there smile.

"Thank you, Jaxon." Taking one last deep breath, she continues. "When I came to, we were somewhere new. I wasn't in the trunk, but in a basement, I think. It was cold and dirt was everywhere. There were small windows on a far wall and a set of stairs. I was alone, lying on the floor with my hands tied behind my back. After a few minutes,

Adrian and one of his men came down. He was furious, going on and on about how the guy he killed was going to be his ticket into the big leagues. Kept going on and on about how his dad was playing it safe by not taking what someone named X had." Mine and Mav's eyes snap to Xander. Xander stands frozen, eyes wide in shock, before they blaze with fire. I can hear him grind his jaw from here.

Adrian must have been playing a long game now because, from what we gathered, this all happened two years ago. Adrian's father only passed a year ago. We had a mutual agreement and clear boundary lines. We did business in the north while he took the south.

"Anyway, he just kept beating me, hitting, kicking. He was so mad. Then he made his man drag me over to a chair and hold me down. I knew I was going to die. I figured he was going to shoot me or something, but he had something worse in mind. He brought over a cup with two syringes filled with some liquid. He told me if I complied with his punishment, he would spare Amber. She was the only friend he would still occasionally let me talk to when I was behaving. She knew he was abusive but didn't know to what extent, but I couldn't let him hurt her." A sob escapes her throat, and I waste no time pulling Wren into my lap and wrapping my arms around her. She's so tiny, I try not to swallow her up with my size. Mav is gripping the back of a chair so tight his fists are turning white.

"H-he told me to open my eyes and stare at the ceiling, but that's when I smelt the bleach. When I didn't comply at first, he started telling me everything he planned to do to Amber. I knew I would go through hell and die first before I let him hurt her, so I did what he said. He took the syringes and squeezed them into my eyes. I fought, but the damage was done. He beat me more after that and told the man to drive me into the city and dump me." My thick arms tighten around Wren's slight form. I want to wrap her in a cocoon, keep her hidden away and protected. I must have been squeezing too tight because she let out a squeak.

"Shit. I'm sorry, Princess. Fuck." I go to lift her off my lap, afraid of hurting her right now with my anger at what she went through, but she wraps her arms around my waist.

"No. It's okay. Just don't let me go right now, please." Sniffling, she lays her head against my chest.

"Never baby." I tell her and mean it.

"Anyway, I was in and out of consciousness when the guy tossed me out somewhere like I was a piece of trash. Knowing I was going to die, I didn't have the will to fight anymore, but then I thought of Amber. What he said he would do to her. Because I couldn't trust that he would leave her alone thinking I was off dying in a ditch. I chose to fight. I started to scream; I must have screamed for hours. Or at least that's what it felt like until a couple out walking their dog heard me. They called an ambulance, and I was taken to the hospital. They did what they could to save my eyes, but it was too late." A tear slips free, and I wipe it away from her cheek. "The cops came, but I told them I didn't know who I was or what happened. The doctors told them that after severe trauma, short-term memory loss can occur. There was a nice nurse who often came to check on me, and I told her I needed to get a call to someone. I told her I knew who attacked me, but he thought I was dead and that it needed to stay that way. I think she felt sorry for me or something, but she called Amber for me. Amber rushed to the hospital, and she explained to the nurse she was getting me out of town, and the nurse helped sneak me out. The rest is history. Amber helped me heal and get a part of my life back." A small smile graces her sad face at the thought of her best friend. Maybe we can get her to visit Wren soon.

"That's what happened. That's how I know him, and I know he is dangerous." I can hear the plea in her words. The "stay away from him, he could hurt one of you" kind of plea, but she has no idea the amount of blood we have on our hands. And I want to keep it that way.

"He won't be a problem anymore, Wren. I can assure you of that. Once we find the pathetic little weasel, he's a dead man." I glare at Xander and his callous words. Does he not see Wren partially shaking in my arms?

Before Wren can reply or Xander can say anymore, I cut in. "Princess, why don't we go upstairs, and we can lie down for a bit? I'm sure you're exhausted and could use a nap." Xander glares back at me, but I ignore him to focus on Wren.

"Ummm, yeah. I could use a nap, I think." Gripping her body closer to mine, I stand with ease, eyeing my brothers with a look that says, find this piece of shit now. Both men nod as Xander heads for his office to do what he does best: hunt. While Mav heads to the liquor cabinet. I'm sure the asshole will have another few drinks before he can calm down enough not to murder anyone who crosses his path. Hopefully, the house staff knows the look when one of us is on a warpath.

Getting Wren upstairs is a breeze, with her being so light. She burrows into my chest, and something in there flips at the feeling. I hate I know how Wren lost her eyesight, but in a sick, twisted way, I'm glad she did. She can't see me like everyone else does. Women and men alike run from the looks of me. My larger-than-life size and the scar that mars my face tend to add to my scary personality. So, it's somewhat a blessing Wren can't fear me from looking alone. Although I think her other senses are just as in tune, she knows we are dangerous. She can sense it like prey senses the predator in the room, but I think she is overlooking that small fault.

We reach her room in no time as I shoulder open the door and shut it behind us. Heading for the bed, I set her down before kicking off my shoes. "Is it okay if I get more comfortable?" She gives me a small nod, and I strip down to my boxers, then climb in bed behind her. Grabbing the blanket at the end of the bed and pulling it up and over us. I pull her closer to me by the waist, wanting her to feel secure and safe in my arms. Taking in a deep inhale of Wren's scent, I ask, "How are you feeling, Princess?"

She shrugs her shoulders, but I stay quiet, wanting to give her time to process everything. "I feel numb about it. It's been two years since I escaped him, and it almost cost me my life. For so long, I was so afraid of everything, every little sound. Honestly, I just recently started feeling safe, but I think that's because of you three. Don't get me wrong, I think you three are insane, and absolutely dangerous, but another part of me knows you also wouldn't hurt me. That sounds dumb, huh?"

"Not at all, baby, but you're right. I won't lie to you. We are dangerous men. We've killed before and will again." I feel her body shiver at that. "But I can promise you, not one of us would ever hurt you or allow you to be hurt."

"Jax?" She raises her head that has been buried in my chest.

"Yes?" I ask.

She chews on her inner cheek before closing her eyes. "Can you make me forget?" I suck in a breath at her question. She doesn't mean...does she? Her hand comes up and cups my face, right over my nasty scar. "Please. I need you. I need to forget. Replace today with something better." Who the fuck would deny Wren of anything, not me? Without warning, I dive, capturing her lips with mine and tasting her natural sweetness. I shift us so that Wren is laying on her back and start making my way down her body as I lift the shirt she's wearing up and over her head. Her creamy skin on full display, I make my way over to her rosy, pink peaked nipple and suck on it. Wren arches her chest further into my mouth as a soft, needy moan escapes her lips and her hands come up to tangle in my short hair. I continue on down her smooth body, nipping at her skin as I make my way further towards her core. I'm not disappointed when I reach the apex of her thighs. She's warm and wet and already so needy. Wasting no time with teasing me or her, I throw open her legs and shove my head in between, inhaling her essence and drinking in her juices as I lick up her center. She's sweet and my all-time favorite meal. I eat my meal like a man starved, reaching up and twerking her nipples as I go. "Jax. I need more. Please." Fuckkk. Wren saying my name, begging for me, does something to the beast inside of me.

Jumping up, I'm out of my boxers and lining myself up faster than I've ever moved in my life. "Wren, baby, I'm going to make you forget, but I'm also going to make sure you remember you're mine." I don't waste time with any more words. I plan to show her as I slam myself into her. She lets out a hiss of breath at my size, and I give her a second to adjust, leaning in to kiss her lips. "I love you, Wren." There's a hitch in her breath at my words, but I start to move. Sliding in and out as her cunt tries to strangle me as much as it can. It's the best feeling in the world as I fuck my woman into two back-to-back orgasms. I can feel myself getting close as well when Wren wraps her legs around my waist and lifts her hips, causing me to enter her at a new angle and fuck me sideways. My balls draw up as that well-known tingle grows at the base of my spine. "Shit, Wren, you feel so good, baby."

"Jax...." Her moan of my name is a husky purr I want to hear on repeat for the rest of my life.

"Yes, baby......" I ask as I pump faster, chasing that feeling of bliss. I know only this woman can give me.

"Jax... I- I love you too." That's all it took for me to slam home, jet after jet of my seed filling her hot core as her pussy milks me for everything I have.

"Say it again." I demand, feeling beyond cloud nine.

"I think I love you too." This woman has no idea the beast she just chained to her by saying those words to me.

Chapter Five

Maverick

I'm pacing the far side of our home office, debating if I should pour myself another drink. I've already had four, but I'm not numb enough. My blood is already burning with anger and probably doesn't need any more fuel to the flame, but I decide. Fuck it. The whole fucking world can burn for all I care after what happened to Wren. My angel. The more she told us the more I wanted to run out of the room, hunt that fucker down and skin him alive. I plan to do precisely that once Jax comes back down from tucking in our girl.

An earlier moment in the shower flashes in my mind. The way her head was thrown back as I fucked her in the shower. Water racing down her body, tracing the juicy curves she often tries to hide. She looked so relaxed and like she wasn't having a horrible morning, waking up in a cold sweat from another nightmare. We all knew she had them, but never knew what they were about. It makes sense now. The things she told us she went through could break a full-grown man, but Wren fought. Her heart is too big for her chest because even after all that, all the years of abuse and torture, she still fights for the people she cares about. I saw it on her face when she finished her story and told us she knows he is dangerous.

I'm sort of glad she is blind, or else she would see us for the wolves in sheep's clothing that we are. She would have run so far and so fast if she knew what was good for her, but it wouldn't be enough. Not after we've had her. We are the worst kind of monsters, but Wren will hopefully never see that side of us. I know I was an asshole in the beginning, but women are snakes, vipers that, when they finally strike, dig their fangs in to drain you of everything they can. But Wren, I doubt that woman has a mean bone in her body.

I'm at the liquor cabinet, while Xander is on the phone with one of our tech guys demanding answers, when Jax comes strutting into the room. His entire aura screams. I just fucked the life out of that woman. Look at me now. The bastard is basically on cloud nine as he heads over to me, grabs the drink I just poured and downs it before throwing me a smug look and heading to take a seat at the desk. I follow suit with a fresh drink in hand and take the seat next to him. Xander looks up and glares in our direction before returning to his call.

Glancing at the big bastard next to me, I ask. "What's got you in such a good mood? Did you forget what happened to her and who did it already?" The smile drops from his face as he sneers at me. I know I'm being an ass and drinking is only going to make it worse, but I can't get the image of Wren lying somewhere in a ditch, battered, and bruised and left for dead. Relishing the pain, I down the whiskey in my hand, feeling it burn my throat. I need the pain right now, to forget what a dick wad I was to her before.

Ignoring my assholeish questions, he shakes his head with disgust. The Jaxon I know returning. "Do you really think drinking right now is such a good idea?" I shrug, but before I can reply with something probably stupid and sarcastic, Xander slams his fist on his desk, causing everything to rattle.

"Find him, or you will be found in a fucking grave." Is all he says into the phone before hanging up and pocketing his device. Turning to us, he glares. "It seems Adrian is in the wind. They can't find the little weasel, but I have all our men on the hunt." He leans back in his chair, a wicked smile crossing his lips. "He can't hide forever."

Deciding I need to be the one to ask the stupid questions today, I down the last bit of my drink. "So, what now?" I look at both men I call brothers. "We just sit on our thumbs and hope he makes a mistake so we catch him? What if seeing Wren alive makes him think he needs to go after her? He already thought he killed her, and if what she said about that night is true, Adrian has had a game plan for a while now." He must have. After his father passed, we sent out condolences and told him we would keep the mutual "peace treaty" that we had with his father in place until we could all meet. Adrian was quiet for months after his father passed, and we didn't hear a word, but we started seeing his men push the boundaries.

Adrian's father ran the West Corporation, a company that deals in advertising. At least on the surface. He did what we do, run a secret underground empire for the shady yet powerful men in our city. Escorts, drugs, weapons, you name it, we probably have a hand in it. We do a lot of transport of goods across the country, so entering this business under the scheme of banking, real estate and investments was too easy. We have properties all over the city, but you wouldn't be able to tell because we are good at our jobs and have loyal men.

Adrian's father was also good at his job, but his empire has slowly been crumbling. This meeting with Adrian we were supposed to have on the night of the gala, was to make it clear, the boundary lines had been crossed and keeping the peace was no longer an option for us. Rumors were that after his father died, Adrian was all too excited to be king of his castle. Whispers of unsavory deals being made and Adrian's greed to have more than he can manage, have reached us over the last couple of months.

Figuring it was a reaction to the grief of losing his father, we gave him time, but we are done waiting. Now, come to find out, he might have been trying to make moves for the last 2 years. The man Wren spoke of, the one she witnessed Adrian kill, sounds like Xander's cousin, Oliver. We kept him out of our business as much as possible, but the kid was relentless. He followed Xander around like a lost puppy most days, but he was a good kid, and we wanted to keep it that way. We thought nothing of it when he told us he was going out to meet up with a friend. That was until we hadn't seen him for a few days. He wasn't answering his phone, and it didn't seem like he ever went home that night. He just disappeared, and days had gone by before we even realized it. That's when Xander made sure we all had a GPS tracker on our phones or watches. Xander beat himself up over having no leads until now.

"No. I have my guys going over Adrian's history, properties in his and his father's name, businesses, everything. We hunt him down. From what Wren said, he doesn't like loose ends and is easily angered. So, let's make him angry. He will make mistakes and we will get him. We can start by going after West Corporation. Burn it to the fucking ground if we have to." He grins, probably imagining just that. Turning to Jax, his eyes narrow a bit. "How is she?"

Jax doesn't even attempt to hide his wide grin. "Satisfied and fast asleep." I bite my tongue in response, since I have no room to talk right now. I fucked her in the shower just this morning, but Xander's eyes flash with fury.

"You thought it was a good idea to fuck her after what we just made her relive!" his voice booms, echoing off the walls as he abruptly stands, looking like he was to jump over the desk to punch Jax in the face.

To his credit, Jax loses the smile as he crosses his arm across his chest. "She needed to feel something apart from what she was feeling. Wren asked me for it, and you both would have done the same. Mav did, in the shower. So don't act like I did something wrong when our girl needed me." He tilts his head up, daring us to challenge what he just said, but he's right. I couldn't deny Wren a single thing if she asked. "Plus, she told me she loved me." Xander and I freeze, a bit wide-eyed, as Jax adopts a smug look now.

He is practically a peacock, flaunting his colorful feathers in male pride.

But just like that, something in me snaps. This woman, this broken little angel, can still find a way to love someone. A man like Jax, and hopefully, me and Xander. Wren went through the deepest kind of betrayal, yet she loves one of us. Men who are probably worse than Adrian. This time, it's me who is up and out of their chair. I can't be here. I need to think, figure out a way to fix my angel's wings. Without a word, I turn to the door and head for the garage, plucking the keys to my Audi RS 5-sport back off the wall as I pass the kitchen. I hear one of the guys call after me, but I don't bother to reply.

I hit the button to open the garage door as I pass the doorway, making a beeline to my car. Once in, I press start and rev the engine. Needing to feel something of my own right now, I peel out of the drive, rocks flying as I go. The gate is already open at the end of the driveway as I zoom through. I do not know where I am going, but I head towards downtown.

Maybe I'll get Wren something nice.

I've been mindlessly driving for over an hour. My buzz is wearing off and every time I think of something to get Wren, I decide it's stupid or realize she wouldn't like it.

Jewelry? She barely wears any now.

Clothes? What if she doesn't like it, or I get the wrong size?

Books? I don't know what she likes to read.

I'm overthinking it all. I know this, but I just want to see my angel smile. After earlier, I don't know if she will for a while. At least not around us. We just made her relive the worst night of her life. Pulling over, I pull to a stop and grab my phone out of my pocket. I have a few missed calls from Xander and Jax and a couple of messages asking when I plan on coming home. Sending out a quick reply saying I'm fine and will be home soon, I pull up the search engine and type in something I never thought I would have before.

What to get a blind person as a gift?

All the usual things you would think of gifting someone pop up flowers, jewelry, clothes, chocolate, but it's all things I've thought of already, and she deserves more than the basics. A noise from across the street catches my attention, causing me to glance up. I parked across the street from the city park and I catch sight of people out enjoying their late afternoon. Families having picnics, couples taking a stroll, people jogging, but what I focus on is a little girl throwing a ball and a dog chasing after it. The girl giggles as the dog grabs the ball in his mouth and races back to her to do it all again. Then, like it was a sign from somewhere flashing neon lights, I have an idea for the perfect gift. A dog.

My next search has me driving across town to the dog training facility I found online. Walking straight up to the front desk, I bypass the person waiting in line. "I need a dog for my girlfriend." The woman sitting behind the desk stares at me before glancing behind me.

"Sir, someone was in front of you." I glanced at the man who was waiting before I got here. "And there is a process to apply for a service dog. If you are just looking for a dog, there is an animal shelter just down the road." I frown at her words.

"No, she needs a service dog." The woman looks around the room looking uncomfortable, probably from my size and don't fuck with me right now attitude.

"Ok, but there are requirements and wait times. I can get you the paperwork to fill out and get the process started." She gives me a weak smile as she shuffles around her desk.

"I would like to speak with whoever owns this place." I don't have time for any of this and rather get straight to the point. She looks stunned at my request, but quickly snaps out of it, picking up her phone and calling her boss. While she's doing that, I turn to survey the room. Posters of people with dogs plaster the wall, all smiling and happy.

"He will be right out, sir." Glancing over my shoulder, I give her a nod and step aside to wait. A few minutes later, a man dressed in jeans and a button up comes out from a door across the room. He looks at his receptionist, then at me before pasting on a friendly smile. He stretches his hand out as he approaches, and I do the same, giving him a firm shake.

"I'm Collen Smith. I hear you're possibly looking for a service dog." I nod. "Why don't we step into my office and discuss the process a bit more?" I give him another nod before following him to the door he just emerged from. Once inside, he heads to his desk and takes a seat. "So Mr.....?"

"Alder." I say, glancing around the small room.

"Mr. Alder. What exactly are you looking for?" He asks as I turn and give him all my focus.

"A dog for my girlfriend. She had a terrible accident about two years ago." I grind out the word accident. "She ended up blind, and I believe a companion would help her feel safer and cope with some possible PTSD." Collen frowns.

"Well, a service animal does many things. From what you have said, your girlfriend sounds like an excellent candidate. We can start the process, but we would need your girlfriend to come in, maybe meet a few dogs and th-."

"No." I cut him off. He frowns, looking confused.

"I'm sorry, what?" he asks, looking a bit nervous now. It could be from me, standing in front of his desk, practically towering over him.

"I'm leaving with a dog today."

"I'm sorry sir but," he starts, but I cut him off again.

"I'm walking out of here with a dog for my girlfriend and everything it might need. If you can do that for me, I will donate 50,000 dollars to this wonderful facility." Collen's eyes widen, his mouth opening and closing like a fish, but no words come out. After a few minutes of no reply, I ask. "Well?"

"Well, ummm, I suppose we could work something out, Mr. Alder. Ummm… why don't we go take a look at a few of the available dogs and see if any pique your interest." And with that, I was on my way to getting our woman the best present ever.

Chapter Six

Wren

I'm still half asleep, not ready to face the guys or anyone, after my earlier confession, when I hear barking. A dog barking. That can't be right, since the guys don't have a dog. After a long minute of listening for clues, my curiosity gets the better of me as I slip off the bed and reach for the robe usually to my right. My fingers touch the fluffy material and I smile. One of the guys learned quickly that I enjoy soft, fluffy things. Slippers, socks, pajamas, you name it, if it's soft and cozy I want it. My bet is on Jax since he is basically a giant teddy bear when it comes to me. Pulling on the robe, I tie a knot around my waist and head towards the noise. I make sure to keep my steps quiet as I descend the steps, the barking noise getting louder as I go.

"Will you keep him down? Wren is asleep and needs her rest. Why the hell did you bring this mutt home? One second you're saying you just need a drive, then hours later you bring home this, without even talking to us," Xander sneers. I can hear the disgust in his tone as I pause, pressing my body into the wall. If my sense of direction of the house is correct, I believe the guys are in the living room.

"He's not a mutt, he is a pure breed German shepherd, and I got him because he is a service dog. He is for Wren." Maverick responds. "Isn't that right? You're a good boy, huh? You'll protect our girl and keep her safe when we have to go to work, won't you?" I almost let out a giggle at Maverick's baby talk to this supposed dog. The man is usually as gruff as Xander. This is a side of him I've never experienced, and I'm not sure how I feel about it.

"You don't think she has enough going on? You had to add a dog to the mix. What if she's allergic or doesn't like dogs? You don't think sometimes, Mav." Xander exclaims, sounding a bit on edge.

"Maybe she will like him. If he is a service dog, then he is trained to help people like Wren. He could help her get around," Jax speaks next. He sounds a bit more up to the idea, making me smile. Since I've known these men, Jax has always been the one to make me smile. Doing everything he can to do it.

"She has us to get around. I'm not letting her leave this house. Not until we find that bastard, Adrian." Xander's words feel like a slap to the face. Who the hell does Xander think he is? Thinking he can just command me to stay in this house. That I'm some kind of pet he can tell to sit and behave. That's not going to happen.

I'm about to turn the corner and give Xander a piece of my mind when a cold wet nose bumps my hand. I startle, letting out a squeak when I feel a furry head bump me next. It's the dog. I hear footsteps heading in my direction, but I'm too annoyed with my stupid controlling men to give them my attention now, so I drop to my knees and stick out my hand for the dog to sniff. The furry head nudges my hand again in what I'm guessing is approval, so I lean forward, sliding my hands through his fur and finding his ears, giving it a few good scratches. The dog instantly bows his head more to give me better access.

"Awww, do you like that boy? Does that feel good?" I coo. In answer, the dog drops to his belly and lays his head on my knee. "I think you do."

"I agree with Xander now. She doesn't need a dog. She is going to give him all the love and attention." I can hear the pout in Jax's words, and I let out the giggle I held back earlier.

"Why is there a dog in the house, anyway?" I ask, even after hearing Mav say it was for me. I move to sit on my butt, but arms scoop me up bridal style.

"Come sit on the couch, and I'll explain." Mav carries me to said couch before sitting with me in his lap. I hear the click, clack of dog nails on the hardwood floor before the seat next to us dips and a furry head lands in my lap.

"Get the fucking dog off the couch!" Xander exclaims, but I ignore him and continue my petting session with a grin on my face. I hope it pisses him off because I'm also pissed at him.

"I think she prefers him with her already." I can hear the smug response in Mav's voice. Shaking my head at the overgrown children, I wait for an explanation. "Why don't you get a drink, brother, and calm down a bit? Wren seems to like him, and I can explain my entire reasoning." I hear a low hum before the clinking of glasses and liquor being poured.

I nuzzle deeper into Mav's lap, chasing his warmth, when I hear a sudden hiss of breath against my ear. "You keep rubbing up against me like that, and we've going to have something better to talk about." He whispers, nipping at my ear as he reaches between us and readjusts himself. Oops.

Deciding its best not to go there right now, I focus back on the furry body nudging me with his head for more pets. "What's his name?" I ask as I give in and scratch behind the dog's ears again.

"Well, his name is Ares, and he's a 1-year-old German Shepard. They were getting ready to send him to a shelter because he couldn't pass all his training." I frown at this, but before I can ask what training, Xander is opening his big month.

"Wow. You couldn't even get her a real trained dog. You got a dropout, and a young one at that. What good is he, then? If he shits in the house, you're cleaning his mess-up." He growls out the last part. Someone woke up on the wrong side of the bed.

"He is trained enough. He was being trained for the police academy program, but apparently, he never caught on. They said he was well-behaved for the most part. He knows commands, and the trainer said he catches on quickly, so training him further for Wren's needs shouldn't be a problem." As if Ares knows we are talking about him, he lets out a chuffing noise. "Look, I know we all want to keep Wren safe, but if it's not clear enough, Adrian is after more than our woman. We can't keep her locked up, and before you say anything, Xan, how about we ask Wren what she wants?" When no one says anything after that, I realize

Maverick is serious. He wants to know what I think about this situation.

Honestly, I'm a bit too shocked to even answer the question. These men haven't cared once what I thought about this last month. No, they kidnapped me and told me I had a month to "get to know them". I was told to give them a chance, and now Maverick was asking for my opinion. The man didn't even want me here at first, and now he's the one advocating for my wants. What kind of twisted alternate universe did I wake up in?

"Angel." Mav whispers, his hot breath caressing the side of my face. "Tell us what you want. I know a lot has happened in your life over the last month and most of it has been out of your control, so how do you want to move forward?" He's right about one thing. This last month has been completely out of my control, and it feels like it's just been one thing after another, but I know one thing for sure. I will not roll over and hide, not anymore.

Taking a deep breath, I decide its time I take my life back.

I'm fresh out of the shower and sitting at my vanity when Abby enters the room from my walk-in closet. "OMG, Wren, I would kill to have your closet as my own. It's basically a high-end retail store in there."

I giggle at that, since I have no idea what is actually in my closet anymore. "You're more than welcome to borrow whatever you want. I am pretty sure I don't know what half of it is, since the guys had someone buy most of it."

Abby lets out a shriek of excitement. "No way. I love you already because whoever bought that wardrobe has great taste." I feel her set down something next to me, the fabric soft against my arm. "Oh, I found the cutest baby blue dress that is so you. It says, I'm sweet but also ready to get down to business. Perfect for your first day back. Are you excited?"

Nibbling on my bottom lip for a second, I debate how I should answer. Deciding to go with the truth, I let out a deep breath. "I'm excited to be back at my shop. It's been forever, but I'm actually super nervous. I know the guys don't want me to go back yet. Not until they find Adrian, but I'm tired of feeling so afraid, so trapped. I want to get back to my old life."

"Wren, you know the guys are only worried about you. I've only known you and them for a short time, but it's completely obvious they are obsessed with you. They just want to keep you safe, but I also get you wanting some space, too." Abby leans forward and wraps her arms around me in an embrace. I have to breathe through the tears, wanting to fall from the sheer sweetness that is this woman. I'm so glad I gave her a chance. The only other person who has ever given me a hug like this is Amber, and with her across the country right now, I didn't know I needed another girlfriend. "I know it's hard, but meet them halfway, Wren. They are just afraid to lose you." She pulls away after that. "Now, go get dressed, so I can work the rest of my magic. We have an hour before we need to leave."

I do as I'm told, heading for the bathroom before slipping in and closing the door behind me. I take a second to get my emotions under control. The frustration with my men and Adrian not having been found yet feels like this overbearing weight on my chest. I want to scream at the top of my lungs to release it all, but I don't. Instead, I take a few more breaths before getting dressed. I pull up the pants, buttoning the clasp before pulling the shirt over my head. The fabric is soft against my skin, unlike anything I've ever owned prior to meeting the men. I slide my hands down my shirt, making sure everything is in place, and step back out into the room.

"I knew that color would look good on you. Now come over here and let me work my magic. Not that you need it." If I could roll my eyes at her, and she could see them, I would. I take my seat and let her get to work, brushing on whatever makeup she sees fit to use before she brushes out my hair.

It's weird having someone who now does all the things I couldn't do on my own. Before, I would simply run a comb through my hair, then throw it up in a messy bun and pray it didn't get too tangled. Makeup was a rare occasion, and Amber usually helped with that. My outfits consisted of leggings, jeans, and a few nice shirts. Nothing fancy, just comfy and easy to move in.

After about twenty minutes, Abby is putting on the last few final touches. "Annnnnd done. Voilà." I give her a smile before standing.

"How much time do we have?" I ask, heading to the bed where I left my shoes. I went with simple flats today, knowing I have a bunch to catch up on today at the shop and will most likely be on the go today.

"About 30 minutes. I'm going to go get ready and meet you downstairs. I think the guys are in the kitchen with Marie, if what I'm smelling is any indicator." At her word, I take a deep inhale, the smell of bacon and something sweet filling my nostrils. My stomach lets out a growl in protest. Abby lets out a giggle and I follow suit.

"Good idea. I think I need to eat before we go." I hear Abby's soft "okay" reply followed by footsteps leading to the door and a second later I'm alone.

Yesterday's conversation with the guys about me going to work pops up into my mind. Xander being upset at the fact I didn't want to stay home and be pampered all day. Jaxon grumbling about how Ares was now getting all my attention, and Mav being all smug that I actually agreed with him. The conversation ended with Xander storming out, saying he needed to punch something, then Jax telling me he was going to find me an even better gift.

I'm pulled from my thoughts when I hear a soft whine. I snap my head in the direction of the door. "Ares?" I call out and a second later, a big furry head lands in my lap. "Hey there, boy. Ready to get to work?" A wet, slobbery lick follows my words. "I'll take that as a yes." I stand, patting Ares on the head. "Well, boy, let's go face the three big, bad wolves."

Chapter Seven

Wren

Ares stays at my side the entire way to the kitchen. His body pressed against my legs with a steady pressure that is reassuring and kind of adorable. I can already tell Ares will be a wonderful dog for me. As we approach the kitchen, I can hear the guy's not so whispered conversation about me. I swear, some days, they think I'm deaf and not blind.

Deciding not to take their shit today, I straighten my back, take a deep breath and charge forward, head held high. Just as I thought it would, their conversation cuts off as they hear me enter. Men. "Good morning." I call out, reaching forward to feel for the kitchen island.

Warm skin meets mine a second later as Jax's enormous arms wrap around me. "Morning Princess. How did you sleep?"

Giving him a bright smile, I allow Jax to lead me to a chair. "Good." I lie. I slept horribly and I know he knows it, but I have to show them I need to do this. "What's for breakfast? I'm starving." My stomach chooses another ill-timed moment to let out a growl that could rival a bear.

Jax chuckles next to me before I hear the soft ting of a plate being set in front of me. The smells from before are ten times stronger as I take a deep inhale, savoring the scents. "Marie made the work's baby. Bacon, banana pancakes, scrambled eggs, and some fresh sliced fruit." I can feel myself practically drooling as he lists off everything.

"Oh, and don't forget this," Mav calls out from my other side. Moments later, the smell of freshly brewed coffee fills my nose, and I sag in relief.

"Yessss. I knew you were my favorite." I say sweetly as he places the hot cup into my hands. It smells even better up close as I slowly bring the rim to my lips and sip. The bittersweet taste of coffee and hazelnut creamer fills my taste buds, and I let out a moan of appreciation. "That is amazing!"

"Why is he always the favorite?" Jax whines, making me giggle. I swear, the man is a giant teddy bear who only wants to cuddle and hand feed me like I can't do it myself. From what I know of him, he is a beast of a man. I can feel his corded muscles when he wraps me up in his massive embrace. You wouldn't think a man of his size would be sensitive and need extra morning snuggles to start his day off right. Big baby.

"You can be my favorite too, if you tell me what you three were talking about before I walked in a few minutes ago?" I don't wait for a response as I set my coffee down and feel for my fork. I don't bother figuring out what food is where, and just go for it. Stabbing my fork down and scooping up whatever it hit. Eggs and a bit of pancake if my taste buds are right.

"It wasn't anything bad, Little Bird. We were just readdressing how best to handle you wanting to go back to work today." Readdressing? Wasn't anything bad? What does he think I am, stupid? I may not have known these men all my life, but in the last month, I've learned a thing or two. What I know is Xander doesn't enjoy being told no, and that's exactly what I did yesterday.

No, to a ten-man security team.

No, I wouldn't wear a damn GPS tracker.

No, the three of them couldn't come to work with me.

I grind my teeth, trying not to scream at him, but he makes it really hard. "Xander, we already talked about this.

I'm not hiding away like some damsel in distress. I want to go back to work. Please." My voice almost breaks on my last word. It is coming out more like a plea. He needs to understand that I need to feel normal right now. I take a deep breath, getting my emotions under control once more before opening my mouth to plead my case again for the hundredth time, but the heavy hands on my shoulders give me pause.

"Little Bird, please hear us out." When I stay quiet, Xander continues. "We have talked more about this subject and have come to an agreement. One we would like you to think about." He pauses, probably giving me time to rebuke his words, but I continue to keep my mouth shut. I know all he wants is to keep me safe, so I suppose I can hear him out. Picking up my fork, I scoop up another mouthful and take a bite. Xander takes this as his cue to continue. "All we want is to keep you safe, and right now, we don't know what Adrian is up to. We understand you need space and want everything to go back to normal, but it can't. Not yet. So, you said no to the security team and us going to the shop with you, but what about a compromise? What if we send two men with you and one of us is allowed to accompany you?" I'm about to tell him absolutely not, but Jax jumps in.

"Princess, please. The two guys would also be there to keep Abby safe. They will be more of a driver and watchman. They can stay outside and be there for when you need them. Us going is for our peace of mind. One of us has been with you at all times for the last month. We don't want to risk Adrian thinking he can make a move at you to hurt us. And I promise we will behave and just work from your office or the side or something." His voice is low and calm, but I can hear the tinge of desperation in it. They really need this and he knew bringing Abby's safety into this would crack my resolve. Damn him. I would never forgive myself if anything happened to her.

Knowing I've been beat, I let my shoulders sag. Letting out a dramatic sigh, I give the guys what they want. "Fine, but only one of you is allowed to stalk me a day and if I feel you're hovering or scaring away customers, the deal is off. Do you understand?" Three rounds of "yes" sound around the room. "Oh, and Ares gets to come, too." I hear Mav chuckle, but Jax and Xander both groan. Too bad they will have to get over it.

A body leans against my back, Xander's warmth flooding my system. The soft tickle of his lips brush against my ear, his hot breath caressing my skin. "Thank you, Little Bird. Now finish your breakfast so we can head out." He kisses the top of my head before fully pulling away. I miss his warmth for a minute before the excitement of finally going back to work fills me up. I practically shovel the rest of the food into my month as my men go about their mornings.

A few minutes later, Abby enters the room, a bright ray of bubbly sunshine. "Good morning, everyone. Have we figured out how this will all work?" Her voice is light and airy as I hear her pour herself a cup of coffee.

"Yes. I'll be accompanying you two, along with two of our men. Oh, and this is for you." Xander says, his tone for once not sounding ice-cold.

"A new phone? But I have one already."

"Yes, but this is an upgrade. Plus, it has all the numbers you could possibly need to contact one of us. I've also ordered you a credit card, it should be here tomorrow. It is to be used for anything you think, Wren, or you may need. Anything at all." He continues like he didn't just drop a bomb on her. I'm a little shocked by his words myself.

"Oh, I won't need anything but my regular pay, sir." Abby sounds a bit lost now.

"Nonsense. You will use it for anything you want. Think of it as a bonus. Plus, you have already shown you are a loyal person and Wren really enjoys your company. So, it's also a thank-you gift." Mav jumps in this time, and I can hear the smile in his words. He's not wrong. Abby has been an absolute sweetheart since I met her.

"I'm not taking your money for being a decent human being. That's ridiculous." She retorts. I could totally hug her right now. If only she knew what her kindness actually meant to me. Being blind means a whole other struggle with people just being rude or flat out ignoring you. Some even think it's contagious or something.

"Abby. Please, just take it. Trust me, it's not worth arguing. It gets you nowhere. Plus, we can plan a shopping trip soon." I can almost hear the eye roll she gives me.

"Ugh. Fine, you win this one. You about ready to go?" she asks and I perk up like a damn prairie dog.

"Ekk. Yes. So ready. Let me grab my bag." I slide off the chair, reaching out until my hands reach the cabinet lined wall. No sooner do I take a few steps than Ares appears, pressing his body against mine. I'm turning the corner when I hear Maverick speak with a smug tone.

"See. I told you he would be good for her. He hasn't even left her side since they met."

The scent of old books, ink, and freshly brewed coffee assaults my nose as I enter the Cozy Nook Bookshop. It's like coming home after a long vacation as the ding of the bell rings above me. "Hi, welcome in. Can I- Oh. Mr. Ashford, this must be Miss St. James." I hear a masculine voice come out from the other side of the shop. Ares lets out a low growl and steps in front of me, causing me to reach down and run my fingers through his fur.

"It's okay Ares." At least I hope so, since the voice I just heard wasn't familiar. Xander next to me mumbles something that sounds like, "Maybe the dog is good for something." But I can't be certain.

"Oh wow, Wren. This place is so cute. Mind if I browse a bit?" I let out a giggle at Abby's words. What I wouldn't give to experience being able to see entering a new bookshop. I used to love running my fingers over each shelf and each spine of every book, reading the titles as I went. Now I can do only one of those things.

"Of course. Go wild." As she heads off to explore, Xander places his hand on my lower back and motions me forwards with a tap. I pray no one moved any shelves or stands in my absence, but as we go, everything feels right.

"Wren, this is Mr. Barron. He helped manage the shop while you were out." As if he can sense my unease, Xander adds. "I gave strict instructions that nothing was to be moved or changed while you were out. He just helped Caleb and Camille open and close. He also dealt with all the financials and bank runs. Everything should be in order, as I oversaw that as well."

"Yes. It's been my pleasure. I can review everything with you if you would like. Mr. Ashford made sure everything ran smoothly while you were out. There were no problems at all." I can feel my whole-body slump in relief. A small part of me thought I would come back to a whole new bookshop or something worse, like it burning to the ground.

"Yes. I would like a quick run-down if you wouldn't mind."

"First, I have one thing to show you. It's a recent addition to the shop, but I think you will benefit greatly from it." My stomach drops. I don't do well with change. Xander leads me over to the front counter and around to the back of it. "Place your hand on the keyboard." I frown at the odd request but slowly bring my hands up and onto the said keyboard. As soon as my figures touch the cool plastic, I'm gasping in shock. I trace all the bumps and grooves and realize it's all in braille. It's a braille keyboard. I'm completely stunned. I'm speechless. My eyes start to tear up at the fact that Xander would think of something like this. "That's not all. It's connected to a voice command computer and printer that will print in braille as well."

"You did this?" I ask. My emotions have been all over the place this week. One second I want to scream at these men and the next I just want to cuddle up in their lap like a damn cat needing attention. But this, no one has ever tried to go out of their way to make my life easier.

"Of course, baby. Mr. Barron here did the research, and we made sure to get everything set up and ready for your return. Do you like it?" he asks, and this time I don't bother trying to hide my tears.

"Yes." I turn and throw myself into his chest. My arms wrap around his waist as he returns the motion. "Yes. This is amazing Xander. Thank you."

"Anything for you, Little Bird. Now I'll let you start your day. If you need me, I'll be in your office, as promised. Okay?" I nod dumbly against his chest, not yet ready to let go. He lets me hang on for another minute until I finally step back and wipe my face of all wet and salty evidence of my crying.

"Thank you, Xander. This means the world to me." He simply kisses the top of my head before leaving me to my first day back.

I have no idea how long it's been since we got here, but Mr. Barron and I have gone over everything that's happened in the last month pertaining to the shop. Apparently, the shop is doing better than I thought because sales are up since I last reviewed them with Amber. Ares hasn't left my side since getting here, and I couldn't be more surprised. Abby even tried to take him for a walk, but apparently, he did his business, then whined to come back in. To say he isn't already protective of me is an understatement.

"Well, that's everything, Miss St. James. I'll be on my way. If you need anything else, Mr. Ashford can get a hold of me." We say our goodbyes and I thank him again as he takes his leave. I am barely about to grab a coffee from the back when the front door rings.

"Good afternoon." I call out.

"Good afternoon, Princess." Jax replies. A smile lights my face as he wraps me up in his big arms.

"Hey, don't hog her. I missed her too, asshole." Mav growls before I'm being pulled out of my big bear's arms and into Mavericks. "Hey Angel. How's your first day back?"

"Exhausting, but that's just cause I don't like paperwork." I lean against Mav's chest, my ear laying across his heart, the sound of it thumping away, calming to my nerves.

"Me too, sweetheart. You hungry? We bought lunch." I pop up at Jax's mention of food.

"Starving. I knew you were one of my favorites." Mav snorts at my words as he leads me to the back, but before we make it very far, the front door rings again. I almost let out a groan before I remember this is my shop, and I wanted to come back today.

"Miss Wren?" A small voice calls out.

"Miss Wren, are you here?" A second small voice sound after the first.

"I don't see her, mama." The last tiny voice has me turning in that direction and stepping around the counter, a wide smile on my face.

"Look, it's Miss Wren." Three sets of tiny feet stampede down the aisle in my direction. I barely have time to brace myself, as I'm practically tackled to the ground by my three favorite little bookworms. Michael, Mason, and Mia Williams. "We missed you, Miss Wren."

"Why did you leave?"

"Are you going to read to us again?"

"Where did you go?"

"I've been reading every day. Just like you told me to."

"Whoa. Who are they, Miss Wren?" The last question is a loud whisper as the three tiny terrors finally climb off and I'm lifted from the ground by arms under mine.

I'm flustered at the question, not knowing how to answer the triplets' curious minds. "Well, umm. These are. Well." How do I explain to 5-year-olds that I'm in a relationship with three men? Or that I was kidnapped by said men. That's why I wasn't here. But that the kidnapping turned out to be okay since I'm now sleeping with the men who took me. Oh! God, I'm spiraling. I can't explain that to them. I never thought about how I would have to explain my relationship with these men to people. People are going to call me names, think I'm a horrible person.

I'm about to have a complete and utterly disastrous emotional meltdown when Abby, the saint she is, speaks. "And who do we have here?"

"I'm Michael and this is my brother Mason and my sister Mia. Who are you?" I almost giggle at Michael's firm tone. He has always been so protective of his siblings.

"I'm Abby. I'm Miss Wren's friend and I work with her now."

"Who are they?" he asks again, and my panic rises. Why is this so nerve-wracking?

"Oh, those big guys? Those are Miss Wren's friends too. They do all the heavy lifting for her." Mia lets out a little giggle. Luckily, the triplets have the attention span of all small children.

"Miss Wren, can you read to us?" Mason asks, causing me to relax my stiff shoulders.

"Of course, sweetheart. Why don't you three go pick out some books? We have a lot of reading to catch up on. That way, your mom can run some errands." A chorus of yay's sound before the running of feet.

"Wren, darling, you're a saint. I'll be out for an hour, tops." Mrs. William says.

"No worries. I missed these three." As I hear her walk back towards the door, she calls out to the kids to behave. Arms wrap around my waist before hot breath flutters across my cheek. Jax's scent of gunpowder and a woodsy aftershave fills my noses.

"I'll show you how much I'm not just a friend tonight, Princess. I'll make it very clear where I stand with you." And then he's gone.

"Miss Wren, are you coming?"

My cheeks heat red as my thoughts stray to the gutter. Yes, I will be tonight.

Chapter Eight

Xander

It's been an entire week since Wren has been back at her little bookshop. The guys and I have been taking turns with who goes with her daily. We even started having lunch with her because no one wants to be away from her for too long. Not with the piece of shit Adrian still loose. The little weasel has been clever enough to evade us so far, but his luck will run out. He will make a mistake and we will be there to put the bastard down like the rabid dog he is.

When I find out who has been helping him, they will be on my shit list as well. I've had A.A.L. Banking, mine, and the guy's financial company, liquidate all of Adrian's assets. It's taken some time, more than I would have liked, but piece by piece, everything Adrian West owns will be mine. I only feel slightly bad since his father was a half decent man, but his son dug his own hole.

A text notification pops up on my phone. Checking the time, I see it's half past seven, meaning it's just about time for dinner. I quickly reply to one of my men, letting me know the shipment was running an hour later because of some traffic. It's no cause for concern usually, but lately, it's the little things that have seemed off. Now that we know it's been Adrian messing with our side business, we won't take any chances. I let my guy know I'll be there to receive the shipment tonight and to keep me posted. We've never had one of our men double cross us, but there is a first for everything and everyone can be swayed somehow. Blackmail, money, threats, there is something for everyone.

I figured I've worked long enough that I could use a break, plus it's been a few hours since I've last seen my little bird. Standing, I stretch out my sore muscles before making my exit in search of my woman. I check the downstairs rooms first, the den, sitting room and kitchen before heading upstairs to her room. I knock first before opening her door, but to my surprise, her room is empty. Pulling out my phone again, I text the guys.

"Where's Wren?" I turn back towards the stairs to head back down when my phone goes off. I almost take a tumble down the flight of stairs when I see the pictures Mav sent me. It's Wren in a bikini, laying out in the sun. Another of her swimming in the pool with the damn mutt paddling after, but it's the last one that really gets me. Wren, with her eyes closed, bright white smile, and head tilted to the sun as if she were a flower seeking warmth. The light is hitting her just right, that she practically glows in the setting sun. I didn't think this woman could get any more perfect, but every day I find a new reason to fall for her deeper.

Quickening my step, I hurry to the back of the house, wanting to witness the beauty that is Wren. Even after everything life has put her through, she is a ball of pure light. Always wanting to see the good in people. She has no idea the effect she has on a room. It's hard not to be drawn to her. I reach the back door in no time and catch a moment where Wren is throwing her head back with laughter at something Abby just said. She looks so free and happy. Jax and Mav can't keep their eyes off her, either. It's like no other women exist now that we have Wren.

I make a B-Line to my little bird and scoop her up in my arms. A startled scream cuts off her laugh. "Little Bird, I've missed you." Her body instantly relaxes in my hold.

"Xander. You scared me half to death." She lets out a cute little giggle before adding. "But I missed you too. Are you done with work?" I look over her head at the guys. I give them a look they know all too well. We might have an issue tonight.

"Yeah baby. At least until tonight. Are you hungry? I think dinner is just about ready."

"Argh, Yes! I'm starving. I've been so hungry lately. Let me go change really quick and I'll meet you all in the dining room in like twenty. Okay?" I give her a tight squeeze, holder her tighter to me, not yet ready to let her go, before kissing the top of her head.

"Yeah babe. Don't be too long." Setting her down on her feet, I smack her round, perky ass for good measure. She lets out a shriek before her, and Abby starts to head inside, giggling like schoolgirls. Ares trots along behind them like the attention stealing dog he is.

The moment she is back inside, I turn to the guys. "I have a bad feeling about tonight's shipment. I got word it's going to be over an hour late. Traffic." I scoff. "I bet you it's either another wrong shipment or a missing one. We need to head this off sooner rather than later, or we are going to start losing business."

"Let's head to the warehouse after dinner and straighten a few things out." Jax smirks, and I can only imagine what he might have planned. The man has had no one to play with for a while.

We are barely ten minutes into dinner when my phone goes off, making me grind my teeth in irritation. Abby eyes me with worry before glancing at Wren, then taking another bite of her food. I glance at the guys before pushing away from the table.

"Excuse me. I need to take this real quick." Wren frowns in my direction, but Jax distracts her with a question about the book she is reading. We've learned that it's easy to distract Wren with book talk. Once I reach the doorway leading to the hall, I answer.

"What?" I growl. We were having a nice family dinner when the call came through. I hadn't even got to the main dish yet. So, this better be good, plus the shipment was supposed to be delayed another thirty minutes.

"We have an issue, boss. I think you're gonna want to come down to the warehouse a bit early." The man on the phone sounds nervous.

"What happened?" I peek my head back into the dining room and make eye contact with Jax. I circle my fingers in the air, then use my thumb to point to the garage. He must see that I mean business because the smile he just had drops before nudging Mav. When he sees my look, he turns furious. I don't blame him. Ever since Wren went back to work, we haven't had time to just relax. Someone is always working or is too tired from working. Once I have their attention, I nod to get going. Jax says something to the girls before standing and heading in my direction. Mav walks around the table to kiss Wren on the head. He whispers something to Abby, who nods.

"The truck just showed up a few minutes ago. So I did what you asked and inventoried the shipment, but I can already tell it's not right, Boss." His tone has shifted from nervous to something else. Afraid, maybe?

"How?" I growl. I need him to get to the point, and fast. I turn once Jax is at my side and make our way to the garage. Maverick's footsteps following just behind.

"H-he left you a note." I halt at his words, ice running down my spine and almost causing Jax to railroad me over.

"What do you mean, a note?"

Chapter Nine

Jaxon

Xander races through the streets at top speed to get to the warehouse on the other side of town. From what he told us, it appears Adrian made another move. The coward. Once we realized it was him stealing part of our shipments, we changed everything up. Alternative routes, new lines of communication, even new men. We couldn't for sure say any of our previous men were helping him, since everything checked out. No connections to Adrian or the West corporation. None of the men had out of the ordinary bank deposits and no one seemed in communication with him according to phone records. But to be on the safe side, we gave them new positions within our business.

The normally thirty-minute drive across town took us fifteen as Xander pulls up to the gate. His knuckles turning white as he grips the steering wheel in a tight hold. The gate guard buzzes us in and I can almost hear the grinding of Xander's teeth.

"X, man. You need to calm down. We will get him, I promise, but until then, we need to maintain a strong front for our men. We can't let this bastard get under our skin. Not now. We have too much to lose now." I give him a stern look with my words. He must know I'm right because he eases his grip and takes a deep breath, trying to calm his rage.

"You're right. We have to play this carefully. Adrian could have eyes where we least expect it." He pulls into our normal parking spot on the side of the large metal dark gray building. "Now let's go see what we are dealing with." With that, we all step out of the SUV. I crack my neck from side to side and swing my shoulders around a few times to stretch those muscles. I have a feeling I'll need to do a small workout tonight.

"Jax." Mav calls out. I turn and focus on our task as I go to follow my brothers. Thoughts of my fist pounding into someone's flesh adds a pep to my step. It's been a while since I've given someone a good bloody beating. I've been too wrapped up in my princess to really care, but with the news Xander gave us about this shipment, I'm eager to beat the living shit out of someone now. And someone will get a beating.

We enter the extensive building from the side and head straight for the office near the back. This is where we meet Bobby. He stands at the door, arms crossed over his chest, a nervous look in his eyes. Bobby has worked for us for a few years now. He's a good man in his middle twenties with short, brown hair and bright blue eyes. You would think he was an all-American guy, if it weren't for him being covered in tattoos.

"What do we have?" Xander demands, and Bobby jumps to attention, throwing his thump back at the door. He gives us the rundown.

"The truck pulled in about thirty minutes ago. Everything seemed normal until I opened the back." He turns and heads for the large semi-truck park next to us. "I opened up the back and found the top of one crate knocked off. I thought it was odd, but every once in a while it happens. So, I climbed in and found this inside the empty crate." He hands Xander a folded-up piece of paper. "I double-checked the rest of the crates and found half the guns missing. But it makes no sense. Why did they only take half?" he asks out loud, but I don't care. I focus on Xander, who scans the note before passing it to Maverick.

He proceeds to read it, letting out a slur of curses before passing it to me. I try to tamp down the fire burning in my chest at what I might read, but it's a lost cause as I take the paper and what I notice is a picture attached to the bottom.

I can't believe my eyes at what I'm seeing. The picture is obviously an older one, but it causes the intended effect. A dark hungry beast roars inside my head at the sight of Wren, naked and tied to a chair, battered and bruised. What really causes the rage is Wren's stunning blue eyes being held open with eye retractors. That's when it hits me. This was probably the night the bastard tried to take her life. I don't want to look away, but force myself to read the words written on the paper.

> Isn't my dolly pretty? She bled so pretty and behaved so well. I never liked sharing my toys, so when I was done playing with her, I threw her away. Had to make sure no one else would want a broken little thing. Seems my dolly didn't know how to stay dead. Since she's still alive, I want my toy back. She was always my favorite.
>
> I'll make you a deal. Hand over my dolly and I'll leave your shipments alone. If you don't, it will only get worse. You have a week.
>
> —A

I'm vibrating with anger as I finish reading. "He thinks we would just hand over Wren and take his word. Who the fuck does he think he is? I'm going to kill him with my bare hands. I'm going to skin him alive over a period. Make him suffer for even thinking of Wren again." I grind out. Thoughts of all the ways I could torture this man. Cause him so much pain he passes out, before waking him and doing it all over again. I'll have Doc on standby so he can patch him up just enough to live, over and over and over. Adrian West will beg me to kill him, to put him out of his misery by the time I'm done with him. He will know what real pain is, and I'll start by taking his eyes, like he did my princess.

"I think it's time to talk to the driver. See what he has to say." Xander calls out, already making his way back to the office.

Mav's hand grabs my shoulders and squeezes. "We're going to get him, J." Then he's gone, following Xander. I glance down at the photo once again. Wren looks so afraid yet, almost like she knew it might have been her last day to breathe. The thought of her going through that or anything else that twisted fuck can think of has me turning on my heel and storming to the office. The driver is going to give me answers and if I don't like what I hear, I'll kill him.

I'm not even to the door when I hear a solid fist hitting flesh sound. "How long have you been driving for us, Evan?" Xander's work voice is back. The one that drops all emotion, cold, icy, and dangerous.

"T-Two years, Mr. Ashford." Evan mumbles. His eyes are downcast to the floor as he sits in a chair in the center of the room. Evan is a young guy who has worked as one of our long-haul drivers for two years now. He has always been on time and never made mistakes until now. From the nervous posture and sweat beading on his brow, I think he knows he made one of the biggest mistakes of his life.

Maverick steps in front of Evan, blocking his view of me. "Why were you late?" That's what we really want to know.

"There was an accident on one of the back roads I take. Some truck hit a deer or something. Ran into oncoming traffic and caused two other cars to crash. Had to wait for tow trucks and a crew to clean the debris." Evan glances up at Mav before shifting his eyes to Xander leaning against the wall. When his eyes continue to search the room, I step up next to Mav's side. Evan's eyes widen in fear before shooting back down to the ground.

"Now, Evan, why don't I believe you? I told you when I walked in and gave you that first warning hit. If you tell me the truth, you'll walk out of here alive. If you lie to me, you'll be leaving in a body bag." Xander casually calls out and I watch as a full-body shiver of what I'm guessing is fear wracks though Evan's body at the promise.

"I s-swear, Boss." I'm done with the games, the lies, all of it. I lunge forward and land a hard punch to Evan's face. It was so fast and unexpected that Evan goes flying backwards off the chair.

"Then why the fuck is half our shipment missing and a note threatening our woman left in its place?" I roar before sending a kick to his stomach. I was smart enough to wear my steel toe boots today. The punch and kick must have been effective because a second later, Evan is rolling over onto all fours and spitting up blood. I grin as his blood paints the office floor.

"O-okay. Okay." The coward on the floor raises his hand in surrender before reaching for the chair. I kick it to him and he uses it to pull himself up.

"Did that jog your memory about what happened?" Xander asks, and I grin wider.

Once Evan has his ass in the chair, he looks up. Blood runs down his face from his nose to his lip and downward towards his neck. I think I broke his nose and busted his lip. "I-I got a call yesterday. Right after, I picked up the crates. At first, I thought the request was coming from you, but that made little sense. You've never changed the route or orders before, so I hung up and was about to call one of you when he called again." Evan spits some blood on the ground and wraps his mouth before continuing. "The guy offered me 50K to just make a ten-minute pit stop outside the city. Boss, my mom's sick and her medicine is expensive."

I growl at his weak excuse. He could have come to us and asked for a loan or for extra hours. We aren't as heartless as we like people to believe.

"What happened at the pit stop? Where did you stop? Who did you meet?" Xander rapidly fires out questions. His irritation getting the better of him.

"I didn't meet anyone. I pulled over at the rest stop on the east side about twenty minutes from entering the city. The guy told me when I got there to go to the bathroom. That a black duffle bag would be in the last locked stall. If I wanted to keep the money, I just needed to sit there for ten minutes, then I was free to go. I waited and when I came out, I checked the truck, but nothing looked wrong. The lock on the back was still in place. I figured it was just to delay my delivery." Evan's eyes are shifting from one person to the next, probably worried about who might attack him next.

"You never saw the guy?" Mav asks, glancing at Xander then me. The silent communication is clear as can be. Evan has no more information that we need, which means he is of no use to us anymore.

"No, I swear. It was all through the phone. I don't even know how he got my number. Here you can have it to check for yourself. Maybe trace it." Mav takes the phone and steps back to go through it. Xander steps forward with a hum of consideration.

"You could have come to us, Evan. I'll make sure your mother gets the money, but your services are no longer needed." Xander gives me the signal, a single nod.

Evan's pleas fall on deaf ears as I rush forward, my fist raised before slamming into Evan's face again. This time, when he falls backwards, I follow him to the ground. Fist after fist landing anywhere and everywhere I can reach. The first few hits, Evan attempted to block, but I'm too fast. I may be big, but I'm sure as fuck not slow. The slap of flesh against flesh fills my ears and soothes my soul as I continue my brutal assault. I can feel Evan's hot blood splash and soak me, but I don't stop. Evan betrayed us by working with Adrian. The thought of Adrian adds fuel to my ever-burning rage, and I hit harder, wishing this was Adrian. Wishing it was Adrian's blood covering my face and arms. I'm so far into the red haze of my anger that I don't even realize Evan is dead until Mav is pulling me off him.

"He's dead, J. He's gone." I hear his words, but it's not until I look down at the bloody mess I've made on the floor. Evan is unrecognizable at this point. His face and skull are bashed in. I glance down at myself and see that I look like a character from a horror movie. My knuckles are torn, bruised and bloody themselves. The thought that Wren is blind and won't be able to see me like this gives me a little sense of relief. I would scare the life out of her if she saw this. Probably never want to touch me if she knew I was capable of killing a man with my bare hands and not bat an eye.

"That's enough, big guy. We've been away from our woman long enough. I just texted Abby, and she said Wren won't go to bed until we are home. So let's go, Mav, you can work on the phone there, and get some men out to the rest stop and see if they can find anything." Xander doesn't even glance at Evan's body, used to the destruction I can cause. He tosses me a small towel and I use it to wipe up as much as possible before following the guys out. Bobby is standing on the other side of the office door as I pass.

"You know what to do." He nods before pulling out his phone to make the appropriate calls.

I'm the last to the SUV, so I climb into the back seat, still attempting to clean up the blood, but I know it's a lost cause. Tossing the towel out the window, I lay my head back against the seat and stare at the roof. Suddenly, I'm exhausted and all I want to do is shower before climbing into bed with Wren to cuddle. Xander starts the cars and peels away from the warehouse. Closing my eyes, I call out, "Let's go home to our woman, boys."

Chapter Ten

Wren

After the guys left saying they had a work emergency, Abby and I watched a movie in the den. I've only known Abby for a few weeks, but she is already turning out to be an amazing friend. Anyone else would think it's weird, a blind girl who enjoys watching a movie when she can't actually see it. But I love imagining the scene, picturing it in my head. It's like reading a book and envisioning it as a moving story in your head. Abby didn't bat an eye when I brought it up. She only asked what genre and what kind of snack I wanted. She and Amber would get along so well.

The thought of Amber causes a slash of pain in my heart. I miss my best friend so much. I haven't talked to her in far too long, since we went from talking daily to not at all. But I know she is living her new life now and I don't need her to worry about me from halfway across the country. I make a mental note to call her this week and catch up a bit. Maybe I'll omit the whole Adrian popping back up in my life.

After grabbing some popcorn, gummy candy and a bottle of wine, we get comfortable on the couch with some extra blankets Abby brought downstairs. Ares got the memo loud and clear because the second I'm comfortable, he hops up and plops down next to me with his head on my lap.

"Ares, you know Xander is going to yell at you if he finds you on the furniture again." As if knowing exactly what I'm saying, Ares lets out a huff before shifting to make himself more comfortable. I let out a giggle and scratch him behind his ears. "Don't worry, I won't let the big scary man hurt you."

Abby lets out her own chuckle. "That dog has a death wish messing with Xander but also you totally spoil him, but I think he's worth it."

"He absolutely is. He has barely left my side since meeting me." I tell her defending my good boy.

I can almost picture her eye roll as she replies. "Anywayssss. What are you in the mood for? I was thinking something, rom-com. What do you think?"

"I think great minds think alike. What are some options?" Abby names off a few and I confess I haven't watched a movie in over a year and wasn't familiar with any of the titles. So she chooses one called How to lose a guy in 10 days.

I'm not sure what time it is when the movie ends, but I know it's late. I'm starting to get worried. I haven't heard from the guys when I hear the telltale sign of tires on gravel. Ares is up and growling in the direction of the door as I stand. A nightmare thought it could be Adrian coming for me flashes through my mind, but Abby relieves my fears with three simple words.

"It's the guys." I waste no time making my way to the front door. I tell myself it's to greet them, but I know I'm lying. I need to make sure they are okay. I hear Abby's footsteps and Ares' click of his claws against the floor follow.

A second later, the front door is opening, and a wide smile paints my face until I hear a sudden gasp come from behind me. "Oh my god, Jaxon, are you okay?" I can hear the panic and worry in Abby's tone.

I snap my head in her direction before focusing it back towards the door. "What do you mean? What's wrong? Are you hurt?" lifting my hands, I reach forward, trying to feel for one of them. I need to touch them, make sure they are okay.

I jump when hands touch mine. Instantly, I'm reaching up to touch whoever's face. Xander. "Little Bird, we are fine. I promise."

"Don't lie to her. Jaxon is covered in blood." At Abby's words, all the blood drains from my face. Blood? His blood? Who's blood? Jaxon sees the panic in my face because he's suddenly in front of me, cupping my face gently.

"Princess, I'm here. I'm okay. It's not my blood. Xander was telling the truth. All of us are fine." He tilts my head up before placing a feather-light kiss on my lips. Who knew Jax could be so gentle? As if he thought I was expensive fine china, he didn't want to break. "Why don't you come upstairs with me? You can check me over yourself after I shower." I'm nodding before he even finished his question.

"And that's my queue. I'll see you guys in the morning. Night y'all." Abby says in a teasing tone before I can hear her footsteps leading away from us.

"Jax, why don't you take Wren upstairs? Mav and I will clean the den, then head up ourselves." With Xander's "request," Jax grabs my hand and leads me up the stairs.

Once we get to the room, I finally ask the question that's been burning to escape. "What happened tonight? Abby said you're covered in blood?" At the mention of said blood, I envision the worst. It takes everything I have to force my brain to stay present and not wander with the hundreds of ways blood could have ended up on Jax.

Jax lets out a long, deep sigh as he pulls me towards the bathroom. "Princess, I don't think you really want to know, and I don't want you to be afraid of me." His voice is low, almost sad sounding. Tugging my hand back, we stop just inside the bathroom. The cold tile sending goosebumps up my legs.

"Jax, I would never be afraid of you. I know you would never hurt me. I may be naïve in a few things, but I'm not stupid. You three aren't just bankers who own a financial company. I've heard the rumors." I take a deep breath and reach until I'm touching Jax's cotton covered chest. From there, I slide my hands up further until my fingers reach the unshaven scruff along his jawline. I expect Jax to remove my hand, like he usually does because he doesn't like me feeling his scar, but I'm surprised when he just stands there. Cupping his face, I make my point clear. "I've always known you three weren't saints. I was there the night we all met. Did you forget the man you beat, then shot? Yes, I was afraid of you all at first, but I've been through a lot.

A part of me knows you would never hurt me. I trust you, Jax, and whatever you say won't scare me away." I let out a chuckle when a thought hit me. "Plus, I'm pretty sure if I tried to run, you three would just chase me down and drag me back." For some crazy reason, the thought of them dragging me back doesn't cause the same inherent reaction I get when I think of Adrian and what he would do if he got his hands on me again.

Jax mimics my posture, his large hands cupping my face and tilting my head up in his direction. "Wren, baby. You are the best thing to ever happen to us. You're right that we aren't just bankers. We all agreed to keep you away from our underground unsavory business, but you have a right to know. We don't plan to let you go. Never, if I'm being honest, but this isn't the first time and it won't be the last that one of us comes home covered in blood." He lets out another heavy sigh, like telling me all this is so much harder than he thought it would be. I keep myself still, and my face calm. "Tonight, I beat a man to death with my bare hands. You see, we are middlemen. We make deals with one person to transfer...goods... to others who can't get them. One of our drivers got a call from Adrian." I tried to keep my reaction blank, but just hearing the man's name causes an innate reaction of fear and disgust. "He offered money to our driver to make a pit stop on his route. He stole half our shipment and left us a note to taunt us." At the mention of the note, Jax's hands tighten on my face before realizing it and apologizing.

"What did the note say?" A part of me has a feeling it's going to be bad and doesn't want to know, but a stronger part of me wants to show these men I can handle the bad stuff. That I truly am done being afraid.

"Princess, I-." he starts.

"Please Jax. I can handle it." At least, I think I can.

"Adrian said he will stop attacking our shipment and business if we simply gave you back to him." He spits out the words, the anger and disgust clear as the day. A shiver of fear shoots through my body, my lungs seizing their movements. I can't breathe. Memories flash through my mind, one after another, of all the times Adrian got his hands on me. The lessons, the punishments, the night I lost everything. I may have survived dying, but I lost more than just my sight that night. "Wren, baby, breath. He will never get his hands on you. Never." I hear Jax's words, but I'm lost in the memory of the pain.

A second later, Jax is slamming his lips down on mine. The motion shocks me back, but takes a moment before my brain catches up to the present. I throw my arms around Jax's neck to kiss him back. This time I'm getting lost in the feeling of passion, lust, and love. Our bodies move as one as clothes start coming off. Jax lifts me with hands gripping under my ass, and my legs automatically wrap around his waist for support. He carries us over to the shower, flipping on the nozzle before stepping in and pressing me against the tiled wall. The contrast between the steaming hot water and icy wall shocks my system for half a second.

"I love you, Wren. I swear on my life I would never hurt you or ever let that piece of shit bastard touch you. You're safe with us, baby." I barely have time to nod in agreement before Jax is sliding his thick cock into my wet center. I moan at the painful stretch as everything from the last few minutes simply washes away, like the water down the drain. Pleasure bursts through me the moment Jax pulls back, then pushes even further in. Teasing in the most blissful way. I toss my head back on another moan as Jax finally fully sheaths himself. "That's its baby. Let me worship you like the princess you are. God, you take me so well. The others are going to be jealous, maybe upset. We didn't wait for them to join." I allow myself to live in this moment as Jax starts to really fuck me.

My climax builds as he slams into me. His thick cock hitting this sweet spot deep within. His steady pace falters for a second at the distant noise of a door opening. "Looks like we are going to have company, baby. So let me have one before they try to steal you from me." Then his pace turns deliciously ruthless. My back slams against the tiled wall as he pounds into me before leaning down and taking my nipple into his mouth. He sucks for a second before he bites down. The sharp and sudden pain causes shutters to race through my body, straight to my core, and like the fireworks on the fourth of July, I explode.

Jax follows me over the edge as he pulls me to his chest, a deep groan leaving his throat. Sexy and low, the sound sends aftershocks of pleasure to my core. I slump against Jax's wide chest, leaning my head on his shoulder, feeling exhausted. I barely close my eyes when I hear one of the others.

"Now, now, Angel. You can't go choosing favorites again until you sample all the goods." I lift my head in the direction of Mav's voice as Jax shuts off the water.

"You're in for a long night, Little Bird."

And just like that, these men replace my fears with something more. Something that, I'm sure, is love.

Chapter Eleven

Maverick

It's been a few days since Jaxon beat our previous shipment driver to death. A few days since, Adrian thought he could threaten us by fucking with another shipment. A few days since Wren found out Adrian still wants her, the sick fuck.

It's my day with Wren at the shop as I follow her and Abby out to the car. Abby takes the front passenger seat next to Edward, the driver and one of the bodyguards for the girls today, while I climb in the back. Wren is already sitting there, looking like the angel I claim her to be. Ares lays at her feet like the good boy he is. I never thought I'd be a dog person, but watching how he took to Wren so fast made me a fan.

Today, she wears a white sunflower sundress that falls to her knees. Her usual flats are gone, replaced by a simple pair of white sneakers. Abby did her hair up in a messy bun that was tied back with something that matches her dress. She also did Wren's makeup in a natural look and light-yellow eyeshadow to pull the outfit together. The sun shining through the window hits her just right that she almost seems to glow as a smile brightens her face. Before I can think twice, I'm pulling out my phone and snapping a quick picture of this moment.

"Are you done staring at me?" At her words, I frown.

"How did you know?" The giggle she releases is per happiness, making my frown and confusion lift instantly.

"Mav, I'm blind. It doesn't mean I don't have a secret sixth sense about things. It's just like I know you took a picture of me. All my other senses are somewhat enhanced." She pauses for a long second before turning to me with a very straight-laced face. Wren leans towards me and over dramatically whispers in a serious tone, "I'm basically a superhero. You know, like the DareDevil." The entire car goes silent before she and Abby break out in giggles. I follow suit with my own chuckles as Edward pulls away from the house.

The car comes to a stop in front of the Cozy Nook Bookshop, while I'm lost in the endless number of emails

I've received overnight. I barely even noticed the drive; I was so lost in work. "Edward, can you go open the shop for the girls while I take them to get some coffee?" He gives me a nod before opening his door and heading out. To anyone else, I'm simply being a gentleman and treating my woman and her friend to coffee before they have to work, but in reality, Edward is clearing the shop for any and all dangers. I'd much rather have one of my men risk their lives than Wren or Abby. And with Adrian still in the wind, there is no telling what he might be capable of if he wants Wren bad enough.

Abby lets out a moan at the mention of coffee. "Yes. Good thinking. I need another one this morning. Wren, babe. I don't know how you got so lucky finding these guys, but they are keepers. I can go grab the coffees. The usuals?" She asks, looking at me for confirmation, and at my nod she climbs out.

"Mav? Do you really think he would try to come after me here? With one of you and bodyguards around?" Wren asks, face turned away, but I hear the fear. Even if she is trying to pretend to be strong in front of us.

"You know him better than us, Angel. Do you think he would?" I ask. Actually, I'm curious about her thoughts.

She thinks about it for a long minute before finally turning to me, a sad look on her beautiful face. "I think when an animal is cornered, all their logical thought goes out the window. All they want is to fight their way out. I knew Adrian was capable of horrible things, but it's been two years. I think he is only capable of worse things now." I watch as a single tear slowly falls from Wren's cheek, but she quickly wipes it away. Before I can reassure her, nothing bad will happen to her and that we will find Adrian. She turns away and opens the car door. Ares jumps out and immediately sits on the curb to wait for his woman. Edward is standing on the sidewalk a few feet back, next to the shop's front door. She must have heard the bell go off after he opened and cleared the place. I want to call her back but decide not to when she pauses, then leans down just outside the car door. "I want to thank you, Maverick. You've always been honest with me. I know we didn't start this, um- relationship- off great, but you've done more for me than I could have ever asked for." She reaches down and scratches Ares behind the ear. The smug pooch gives me a doggy smile, as if to rub it in that he gets more attention than we do now.

"Anything for you, Angel." Is my reply as I climb out my side of the car and head over to the sidewalk. Abby is walking up as we reach the door, a carrier of drinks in her hands and a huge smile on her face.

"Wren, you will never believe it. I think I just met my own prince charming in the coffee shop line." I take mine and Edward's drinks as Abby loops her arm in Wren's, stealing her away to the back for some girl talk, Ares hot on their trail.

If you had told me a few months ago, I would be jealous of a service dog and a pint - size ball of energy woman taking up my woman's attention. I would have laughed in your face. Now, I just follow behind and wait for my chance to have some alone time with Angel.

The guys stop by for lunch as usual before having to head back to the office for more meetings. It's the perk of getting to spend the day with Wren. Abby just ran to get some more coffee for what she calls her "midday slump" when I notice I couldn't see Wren from my spot in the back office. She was just at the counter a second ago and I haven't heard anyone come in since Abby left. Deciding my legs need a stretch anyway, I make my way out of the office in search of my Angel. Maybe I can steal a kiss or two before she shoos me away to get back to work. I check a couple of the aisles, but when I still don't see her, I call out for her.

No answer.

Worry seeps into my mind. It's not possible for me to miss her. Edward and James, who are stationed in the alley in the back, would have notified me if Wren left or if they saw something suspicious. Not wanting to chance it, I head back to the office to grab my phone when I hear something coming from the bathroom. I place my ear against the door and listen for a second, but the sound comes again. Not bothering to wait or knock, I turn the knob to find Wren on the floor next to the toilet, heaving up what she had for lunch. Ares is whining next to her, his big furry head nudging to get her attention. Without thought, I rush to her, but when she sees me approach, a look of horror crosses her face.

"Maverick, what are you doing in here? Get out. You don't want to see me like this." She holds up her hand as if that's actually going to stop me. I grab a few paper towels and wet them before handing them to her to use. She quickly wipes across her mouth and flushes the toilet to hide the evidence I've already seen.

"Babe. We told you we aren't going anywhere. Plus, this is nothing compared to some things we've seen." She sends me a half - ass glare before her body lurches forward to heave up again. Taking a knee, I rub her back in slow, soft circles. "I was worried when I couldn't find you. Then, I got even more worried when I heard you throwing up in the bathroom. Are you okay? Should I call Doc?" I'm about to stand to go grab my phone, but Wren throws her hand up to stop me. She finally stops heaving after a minute and twists to plop her butt on the ground with her head resting on her knees.

"I'm okay. I think I'm coming down with a stomach bug or something. I wasn't feeling great this morning, but thought it was just lack of sleep." She lifts her head and I can see she looks tired and somewhat pale, causing my worry to spike again. Maybe it's something more and I should call doc. "Mav. Please don't worry. People get sick all the time. I'm fine, but I think maybe we can close the shop early. I'm exhausted, and just want to rest." Ares is practically in her lap now, rubbing up against her in an attempt to make her smile.

"Yeah baby. Let's close up and head home." Reaching down, I pull Wren up by the arms, keeping my arm around her shoulders for support as we head for the office. I quickly swipe my phone before heading for the front counter, so Wren can do her closing thing. I send a text to the guys, letting them know Wren isn't feeling well and that I'm taking her home to rest. As Wren closes the register down, the front door swings open, the bell chime, causing Wren to suddenly flinch. Not wanting to upset her more, I say nothing but make a mental note to bring it up later. It's obvious that she is still afraid.

"Sorry. The wind is picking up, and I didn't grab the handle tight enough." Abby calls out. Before she can make it any further, I tell her to lock the door and put the closed sign-up. After she's done, she meets us at the counter with a look of confusion on her face. "What's going on? Is everything okay?"

"Yeah. I'm just not feeling very well. I think I just need to head home and lay down." With Abby, here to watch Wren, I head back to the office to pack up all my work stuff. My phone goes off as I'm heading back, so I check it. A single text and I know Wren is going to be mad.

> Xander: We are on our way.

Just what my angel needs. More overprotective men worrying about her.

Chapter Twelve

Wren

It's been three days since this stupid stomach bug started and I'm so over it. I'm fine all day until bam, out of nowhere, I'm rushing to the bathroom to throw up. The guys have been extra observant of me as well, constantly watching, hovering, insisting they call Doc. I've had plenty of colds and stomach bugs and fought them off all without help from a doctor, so I don't plan to now.

I'm in my room reading a book in bed, since I'm still feeling nauseous, when my phone rings. I reach for it next to me when it calls out Amber's name. We talked for a bit last week but with her new busy life and everything happening here; we haven't gone into great detail about anything. Quickly answering, she jumps right into everything we've missed in the past two months.

She tells me all about her new place and how living with Jacob is amazing. The new coffee shop and yoga studio she found to replace the one she left behind. She even thinks she found the perfect storefront for a new bookshop. She's even met a few new friends from the yoga class, but reminds me I'm her number one bestie for life.

"So, Wren, what about you? How's it been? I've been so worried since I left and you gave me the code phase. Then the next time I talk to you, you're fine and living with three men. How did that even happen? Did they kidnap you or something?" Her words are rushed as she blurts them out all at once.

"Amber. Breathe. I'm..." I try to choose my words wisely, but my extended pause must have been too much for my best friend. Ares must also notice my hesitance because he jumps up on the bed from his bed on the floor and presses up against me. I run my fingers through his furryhead with my hand not holding the phone and smile. He really is a loyal pup.

"Wren! You're what?" She demands.

I blow out a deep breath. No point in lying, since she's always been able to tell. "I'm fine now. It was rocky at first, but I think I'm happy. I know it's unconventional, but the three of them actually make me really happy and with things going on lately, I know they will protect me, too."

I regret the words the moment they leave my mouth. I've said too much, damn it. I didn't want to tell her about Adrian or his threats and promises that he will get me back. I'm hoping she didn't catch on, but I've never been that lucky.

"What do you mean by things happening lately?" Her tone turned from happy and excited to confused and worried.

I really want to lie to her but we promised each other after she showed up at the hospital the night Adrian almost killed me. We would never hide anything from each other again. "Amber, are you sitting down?" I hear a soft thunk before she mumbles a quiet yes. "Before I tell you everything, I need you to promise me you won't catch the next plane back here."

"Wren, babe, you're scaring me." She lets out a weak chuckle like I might make it sound worse than it is and I wish I was.

"Promise me." I demand. Knowing her, she would do exactly what I'm making her promise not to do. But I can't have her here in the city or even the state. Adrian can't know Amber is a weakness of mine. She must hear how serious I am because her next words put me a bit at ease. We have never broken a promise to each other.

"Okay. I promise."

"Adrian is back and knows I'm alive." And just like that, we are on the phone for over an hour. Her cursing, panicking, and telling me all the ways she would castrate the man. Me having to reassure her I'm perfectly safe with my men and hint at the fact they have a more than unsavory part of their lives that makes them capable of protecting me. By the end of me telling her everything from the moment I met the guys in the alley to now, she stays quiet, simply listening and when I finish, she says something I never expected.

"Oh my god, Wren! You lucky bitch. You're living some dark, twisted fairytale. Like Beauty and the Beast, but with multiple beasts. You're Belle, obsessed with reading, and the guys are rich princes who have kidnapped you and now fallen in love with you. That douche Adrian is Gaston, who thinks women should worship him. Ha. That prick dies in the end! Totally a fairytale story." She sounds so matter of fact when she finishes that I'm so shocked, I'm speechless.

After a long minute, I can't help myself. I start to laugh. I'm laughing so hard, tears fall from my eyes. On the other end of the phone, I can hear Amber laughing just as hard as me. My best friend would take a shitty situation and turn it into something romantic. When I finally have my laughter under control, I respond with five simple words. "I miss you so much."

"I miss you too, babe, but it seems like you're finally living for something. You should be proud of yourself for taking a chance. I know it's scary, but I can hear how happy you are now." This time, her words bring tears to my eyes for a whole other reason. Happiness.

We talk for a bit more about random things like new foods we tried, shows she's watching and books I've been reading. I tell her about Abby and she tells me to have a girl's day with her like we used to in the past. Do something like get hair and nails done, then shopping for a new outfit before going out to a club to let loose. I roll my eyes at the suggestion, but the more I think about it, it might be good for me. Plus, Abby totally deserves a girl's day, but she has been talking about updating my wardrobe to something more me. We finally say our goodbyes after our two-hour-long conversation and agree we need to check in more often with each other.

After a quick bathroom break, I go in search of Abby to tell her the plan. Heading to the other side of the house, I find her singing at the top of her lungs in her room. I, of course, wait to announce my presence until she finishes her song and then begins to clap like an enthusiastic crowd at a live concert. She lets out a loud scream, making me cover my ears before the thundering of footsteps can be heard stampeding up the stairs and down the hall.

"What was that? Are you okay?" Jax says, grabbing me by the shoulders and turning me to face him. I'm guessing to look for injuries. Ares lets out a growl at the way I'm being handled, but I make sure to reach down and pat him on the head first before answering Jax's question.

"I'm fine. I scared Abby accidentally."

"Yeah, you did. Damn near gave me a heart attack." She calls out, chuckling to herself.

My cheeks blush at the sudden wave of embarrassment. "Sorry. I didn't mean to scare you, but I also didn't want to interrupt your concert. I was just coming to ask a favor." I turn around in Jax's hold to face Abby's direction. I know the other two guys are here too, but they haven't said a thing yet.

"No worries. What's up?" Her voice sounds closer now.

"Well, I was wondering if maybe this weekend you might want to have a girl's day? Maybe grab some brunch, get our nails done, then go shopping for a few things." A shriek of excitement leaves Abby at my words.

"Yessss. OMG! Yes. I thought you would never ask." Suddenly, small arms wrap around me in a tight hug and the scent of bubblegum fillls my nose. Typical that she would smell like something sweet and bubbly.

"How about Saturday, ladies? I'll make a reservation for brunch and a full work spa treatment." Xander finally speaks and I smile. Of course, he would want to plan out the day.

It's Abby who responds to us. "That sounds perfect. I can call ahead to a few shops and make appointments to get it cleared out for just us. I'll give you the list later today." The two of them talk logistics as Jax spins me around and lifts me off the ground. I instantly wrap my legs around his waist as he heads back across the house.

"I knew I liked that chick. She's taking your safety as seriously as us." I roll my eyes at his cavemen statement and nuzzle my head deeper into Jax's thick corded neck. I doze off in his arms as I remember Amber's words from earlier.

You're finally living for something. And I think I finally am.

Xander didn't want to take any chances for mine and Abby's girl's day. He completely booked some exclusive spa and ordered us the works. Hair, facials, nails, skin, massages, everything a girl can wish for. I have never felt more relaxed and pampered in my entire life. After hours of relaxation, we finally got hungry and left for another fully booked restaurant to have brunch. At the spa, Xander kept his distance, but now I can feel his presence a table away.

Abby and I order some champagne and appetizers while we wait for our main dishes. She tells me about all the shops and styles she thinks I'll look cute in. Throughout our entire meal, we giggle and share stories of our life. She tells me how she grew up poor but always had big dreams, even if she didn't know what she wanted to do with those dreams. I tell her about my life before that prick, Adrian. The entire morning and afternoon feels light and well overdue as we start to finish our food.

"I'm stuffed." Abby says.

"Too stuffed to go shopping?" I ask, knowing damn well she's not.

"Ummm, no. Not that stuffed. I have it all planned out. You ready?" I give her a nod and push back from the table. I'm barely about to sit up when Xander is there, his arm wrapping around my waist and pulling me to him.

Xander's hot breath tickles my neck. "How was your meal, baby?" I suck in a breath at the contact as his lips reach my skin and places a soft and gentle kiss there.

"I-it was delicious. Thank you." My entire body lights up at this man's touch. He guides me through the restaurant to the front, where the car is parked. "Also, thank you for today. I know you probably have work stuff, but I really appreciate you doing all of today." He pulls me up short of the car.

"Wren, baby. I would do anything for you. Any of us would. You deserve all the happiness in the world, and today is the most I've seen you smile all month. I like to see you happy, Little Bird. Work will be there when we are done." As if I could fall for this man any harder, he has to go and be all romantic, like a character in one of my books. This time, I initiate the contact, leaning my head up for an obvious kiss. Xander doesn't disappoint, reading my signal loud and clear as he leans down and our lips connect. It's a tender kiss at first, but I want more. Reaching up, I wrap my arms around Xander's neck and deepen the kiss with all the passion and feelings I'm too afraid to tell him. I'm so lost in the feeling of me wrapped in Xander's arm, I almost jump five feet into the air when Abby loudly clears her throat behind us.

"Sorry to interrupt, but this is still technically a girl's day. So Wren is still mine for a few more hours. Xander, you can have her tonight. Plus, we are late, so let's go." Xander lets out a deep chuckle at Abby's words, and the sound does nothing to calm my damn raging hormones. I release Xander and step back, smoothing down the dress I wore today.

"Sorry. You're right. Where to next?" I ask, trying to focus on anything but wanting to climb Xander like a damn monkey climbs a tree. Luckily, Abby jumps right into talking about this small boutique she found a few years ago.

It doesn't take long to get to the little boutique. Just like at the spa and restaurant, Xander sends two guys who have been driving in a separate car ahead of us to check the shop over. I'm sure to anyone watching this, it makes it seem like we are important superstars or something. I try to ignore the embarrassment, but it's no use. Every time one of the guys does this, I flame red. I tried to explain how this makes us stand out even more, but was promptly told my safety was not to be taken lightly. I tried to imagine what the guys would be like if they were dads with a kid and how they would act, but I immediately shook my head at that thought. There is no way I should be picturing these men as fathers.

A light tap on the window is the signal that the coast is clear. Abby steps out first and I follow. We left Ares with the guys today, since we didn't know how he would handle the spa and shopping. It would be my luck if he decided he didn't like shopping like me and used some expensive material as a chew toy or worse, a tree or a bush.

"Aww, you must be Mr. and Mrs. Ashford." Entering the shop feels like hitting a brick wall of floral tasting air. There is so much perfume coming from the lady who greeted us. I start to sneeze. I don't even have time to correct her greeting. I could kiss Xander right now as he pulls the woman to the other side of the store and Abby pulls me in the opposite direction. The moment I have clean air, the sneezing stops.

"What was that about?" Abby asks before connecting the dots and chuckling, "Oh. I'm sorry. I should have warned you. Miss Dumont, the owner, is heavy-handed with her perfume. Super nice lady, but man, that perfume is a bit much to swallow." I wave away her concern.

"It's fine. I just wasn't ready. You know, since losing my eyesight, all my other senses went into a kind of overdrive, it was a bit much at first, but I'll be good next time."

"Okay. Well, this shop has very cozy and comfy vibes. So why don't you feel some of the material and let me know if you like the feel of any of them while I go grab a few outfits I think you might like?" I give her a nod and reach out, feeling for the rack of clothing while adjusting my purse over my shoulder.

I'm a few minutes in of exploring all the many textures under my palm when I hear my phone vibrate in my purse. Only a selected few people have my number and call me. Assuming it's one of the guys not with me or Amber, I answer. My speaker has been off since the spa, so I didn't get to hear who it actually was.

"Do you miss me, Dolly?" The voice on the other end of the phone causes every muscle in my body to lock as icy fear races down my spine. He found me. My mind struggles to stay in the present as memories of a living nightmare flash through my eyes. "Because I miss you, Dolly. I see you moved on. I thought we were in love, sweetheart. I grieved for you. I thought you were dead, Wren." His words are like strikes of pain across my skin.

"Wh-what do y-ou want, want, Adrian?" I'm trying to be strong. I really am, but it's all so overwhelming. I hear Abby step up next to me.

"Hey, Hey, are you okay?" I know she's there, but the moment she places her hand on my shoulder, my body reacts and I flinch away. "Wren. Who are you talking to? What's wrong?"

Mustering up everything I have left, I whisper, "A-adrian." The sound of footsteps bolting away is all I hear before the man who stars in all my nightmares speaks again.

"Abby is such a pretty little thing. Don't you think? Oh wait, you have no idea what she looks like. What happens when those fuck toys of yours notice her more? When they realize you're nothing more than a hole to bury their dicks in. Why don't you come home? We can put the last two years behind us. I'll even forgive you for opening your legs to multiple men behind my back. What do you say?

I'll even promise to leave your friend alone." His voice hasn't changed since back then. It's still cold, unfeeling, and cockier than ever, but he still knows how to get to me. The mention of Abby has me straightening my spine. I can't let him win this time.

"W-what do you want, Adrian?" This time, my voice sounds stronger until his next words hit me like a bullet to the heart.

"That's easy baby. I want my Dolly back."

Chapter Thirteen

Xander

Watching Wren today has me feeling some new type of way. At the spa, she was relaxed and at ease, a blissful look upon her face the entire time. I watched her from the shadows. Not that I was hiding. She knew I was there, but I couldn't take my eyes off this version of her. At the restaurant, I was only a table away and listened as the girls gossiped about their lives. I learned a lot from just listening.

My little bird had big dreams. She wanted to see the world and experience new things. I noticed how she avoided any conversation about Adrian. The moment you mention him, she completely changes the topic. I can't blame her. Before today, she was still afraid of little things. Mav mentioned he caught her jumping at the sound of her shop's front doorbell. Jax has seen her flinch at the loud noises. And I've seen the way she sometimes stays quiet around the house, almost like she is afraid to make a noise.

From what she's told us about her relationship with Adrian, I can't blame her. He trained her to be afraid of everything. To be seen but not heard. Just the thought of that bastard stirs the rage within. We still haven't caught the slippery fuck. The prick is playing games and I'm getting sick of it. He thinks he has the upper hand, but someone can only hide for so long.

Arriving at the first little shop, Abby planned goes smoothly until we enter and were greeted by an older woman rushing towards us. "Aww, you must be Mr. and Mrs. Ashford." I smirk at the fact I feel Wren tense under my hand, resting on her lower back. That is, until Wren breaks out into a sneezing fit because of this woman, who bathed in old lady scented perfume. You can almost taste the chemicals if you open your mouth. I glance over at Abby and nod to the back of the shop, where all the women's clothes are located. She gets the message because she loops her arm under Wren's and guides her away, and I do the same.

"Ma'am." I start, but am interrupted by the woman who bats her lashes up at me.

"Please, it's Miss Dumont." She reaches out her hand for me to take and I have to stop myself from rolling my eyes at the very obvious flirting going on. Miss Dumont looks to be in her late forties, early fifties. She's taller than my Wren, I'm guessing 5'6"-ish, has reddish brown hair and bright-green eyes. I bet in another lifetime she caught every man's eye. Shit, if I didn't have the most perfect woman as mine already, I might have thought about giving Miss Dumont a go.

"Miss Dumont, my-" I pause for half a sec before deciding to just go with it. I plan to make it true someday, anyway. "-wife hates spending money. Never wants to get herself anything nice. I'm wondering if you might have a jewelry section. Maybe some bags." The smile that lights this woman's face at the mention of me wanting to spoil my wife is almost blinding.

"Now you're speaking my language, Mr. Ashford. Right this way. Was there anything specific you were looking for?" she asks, leading me further back into the store.

"No, but I'm sure I know it once I see it." Across the floor, I spot Abby swiping through racks of clothes and the top of Wren's head close by. Probably doing the same.

I pick out small but simple pieces of jewelry, knowing Wren's not big on it. A few studs or small dangling earrings. Thin chain necklaces and bracelets with small charms. I even found a link bracelet that charms can be added to. I'll have to find unique charms that represent important things in her life. Her shop, love for books, friends, that mutt and one for each of us. I think it would actually be something she wore often. I'll have Abby choose bags to go with whatever outfits they get today as well.

I'm on my phone looking up charms that could work when Abby rushes up to me, worry and a bit of panic in her eyes. "It's Adrian." She rushes out, but I'm already gone. I hit the 2 on my speed dial as I make my way around racks of fabric. Rounding the last of the racks, I spot Wren, phone to hear ear, and face drained of all color. I'm going to kill that bastard.

"What?" Mav answers, sounding annoyed still that I'm the one who got to go with Wren.

"Trace Wren's phone now." I hiss out, then disconnect the call, knowing Mav will do it. All anyone has to say is Wren's name and we would do just about anything.

I make my steps louder than normal, so Wren can hear my approach. Gently reaching out, I grasp her waist, holding the phone. She flinches, and I let out a curse under my breath. "Give me the phone, Little Bird." I watch as her whole body shakes, but slowly releases the phone. The second I have the phone in my head, I pull Wren to my chest and place the phone to my ear.

"Why don't we settle this like real men, Adrian?" I tell him a second before Abby rounds the corner with one of the guards that was with us today. I circle my finger in the air to signal a search of the area. This wasn't a coincidence that he called today or that she was alone when he did. He wants to torment her.

"Now, where's the fun in that, Xander?" The bastard laughs like this is all a joke, only making me picture punching his teeth in or maybe cutting out his tongue.

"This won't end well for you. You know that, right?" I grip Wren tighter to me and can feel her whole body shake. Abby steps up next to me and opens her arms, so reluctantly I turn so she can take Wren into her arms. The moment Abby wraps her arms around Wren, she slowly lowers them to the floor. Smart girl. I might have to give Abby a bonus. Keeping my eyes peeled, I head for the window. I know he's watching, I just don't know from where. Pulling out my other phone, I send a quick text to our group chat.

> **ME: Adrian contacted Wren.**
>
> **MAV: Keep him on the line, we've tracing.**

> **JAX: I'm going to skin that bastard alive.**
>
> **ME: Send more men.**

"That might be so, but I'll be long gone before any of you find me." he lets out another taunting chuckle. "Is her pussy as tight as it used to be? Man, was she a good fuck." Clenching my fist, I dig my nails into my palm. Needing the pain to distract myself, I force myself to not react. That's what he wants, a reaction. For me to make a mistake. "You know, when I first met her, I figured I would keep her around to fuck, then when I got bored, I would throw her back. I never expected to want to keep her, but she was such a good submissive. Easy to bend to my will. I said jump and she would ask how high." Another fucking chuckle. "Then one day she thought she could leave. She thought she could break up with me. That was the first time I had to teach her a lesson. You see, my little Wren is to blame for my issues. The first time I enjoyed hurting someone was her. The way her creamy flesh turned red. The way she screamed and begged me to stop. She showed me how sorry she was all night long that night." The bastard lets out a dreamy sigh, as if remembering all the awful this he's done.

"What's the point of this call, Adrian?" I grind out. His words dig deeper under my skin the longer he talks. It's taking every ounce of strength not to respond.

"My point is that you only have a few days left until Dolly needs to be returned to me. I'm being gracious with the time I've already given you." I'm going to need to see a dentist after today with how much grinding I'm doing. "Has she told you about how she used to moan around my cock while chained to my bed? She used to pretend she hated it, begging me to stop, but she always got wet for me. Those beautiful baby blues staring up at me, tears ruining her makeup, but would still suck my cock like a lollipop. She wanted everything I gave her. Plus, her eyes shouldn't have wandered; it was a shame when we had to finally end things. I was so heartbroken when I heard she had an accident and didn't make it." He mocks, his tone casual, as if he didn't just reference him attempting to kill Wren.

I've held my tongue long enough. "When we get our hands on you, you're going to wish you succeeded at killing Wren. Everything you put her through will be done to you. You will wish for death, but it will never come. I'll keep you alive for as long as it takes to satisfy our revenge and give Wren the justice she needs. You're a coward, Adrian. Not willing to face the consequences of your own actions. So run and hide like the pathetic little rat you are and enjoy the time you have left." My phone vibrates and I look down.

> **JAX: We got his location. Our men are on the way.**

> **MAV: Take Wren back to the office. We need to know what he said.**

Suddenly, Adrian laughs, the sound grating on my ears. "Big talk for someone who can't even protect his own merchandise. Like I said before, you have until the end of the week to return my Dolly, or you're going to have bigger problems." The line goes dead.

I immediately dial Mav. "Did we get him?" my other hand fist Wren's phone. The plastic creaking with the force.

"No." That single word turns what was supposed to be a relaxing girl's day into another nightmare for Wren.

"We're on our way."

After I hang up on Mav, I scooped up Wren into my arms and we made a B-line for the car. The other men I've requested to escort us are already here and waiting. I slide into the backseat, Abby climbing in after me. I keep Wren tight against my chest, her entire body still shaking, and I saw tear tracks staining her cheeks. When she goes to shift off my lap, I pull her in tighter.

"I got you, Little Bird." Looking up, I give the driver a nod, to signal to get us on the road. Wren buries her head deeper into my chest, and I have to force myself not to tighten my grip on her, afraid I might hurt her.

The driver wasted no time weaving in and out of traffic to shorten our drive back to the office. The normal thirty-minute drive only took fifteen. By the time we pull up to the parking garage, Wren is fast asleep in my lap. Abby jumps out and rushes to the other side of the car to open the door, allowing me to step out.

"Why don't you head home, Abby? Wren will be safe with us." She stares at Wren for a long minute, a worried look in her eyes, before nodding and slowly climbing back into the car. I turn back to her. "Thank you, Abby. When we first met Wren, she had only had one friend. She smiles more when you're around. You don't treat her like a burden but a friend. You will always have our protection and we owe you." She glances down at Wren sleeping in my arms and smiles.

"I think you're wrong. She smiles more because she finally feels safe and loved. Wren's something special Xander, I hope you three take care of her." She proceeds to close the car door and drives away. She's right about one thing, Wren, is special.

Footsteps rushing up behind me have me letting out a deep sigh as I turn to face a furious-looking Jax and Mav. Their eyes instantly go soft when the spy Wren still passed out in my arms. "She's fine. I don't know what he said to her, but I think it brought back memories she's been trying to forget. Let's get her upstairs, then we can figure out our next move." I can tell both men want to reach for her, if not to comfort but to make sure for themselves she's okay. Both keep their hands to themselves as we make it to the elevator. The entire ride up is quiet, all three of us just staring at the woman in my arms. To anyone looking in, it would seem creepy, but to us, it's fear that if we blink, she could disappear.

It's clear that Wren is good at running and hiding. She's been doing it for two years. Adrian probably would have never found her if she weren't involved with us.

When we reach the top floor, Jax rushes ahead of us to my office. Once we enter, he already has my couch set up like a bed. We all keep a pillow and blankets in our offices for unexpected long late nights. Gently, I place Wren down on the couch and Mav immediately covers her up. Wren snuggles down into the warmth, and I get my first good look at her face. Her usually soft look is gone, replaced by red rimmed puffy eyes from crying. I place a kiss on the top of her head before heading to my desk, taking a seat and booting up my computer. The guys follow suit, taking a seat across from me, with their chairs slightly shifted to keep an eye on our woman.

"Let's get straight to it. What did we find out?"

"The coward ran before our men could get him. We found pictures of Wren all over the place. It was a small loft apartment about three blocks from where the shop was. It's also about the same distance from Wren's shop." Jax grinds out.

"They also found a couple of computers. It looks like he found a way to hack into some security systems. They saw the spa; the shop you guys were in and the Cozy Nook. We have a guy working on back tracing the IP addresses to see if we can trace him the next time he logs in." Maverick adds.

"What did he want this time?" Jax questions. His grip on the chair is turning his knuckles white. It's killing him that Adrian was even able to get a hold of Wren.

"The same thing he's been asking for. Wren. He says we have until the end of the week before he makes his next move." I run my fingers through my hair and tug. The frustration that he's been able to get away, not once but twice, is borderline insanity. "Let's start making a list of everyone he might work with. Pay whoever you need to extra if you have to. We need to end this now because from the conversation earlier, I have a feeling, if he can't have her, no one can."

Chapter Fourteen

Wren

My head feels fuzzy as I try to focus on waking up. The last thing I remember was curling up into a ball on the floor of the small boutique Abby took us to. Then the floodgates opened as I relived all the awful things Adrian has already put me through. Fear shot through my heart when I remember him threatening Abby. Right in the middle of my breakdown, Xander's muscular arms wrapped around me and lifted me into his chest. I'm almost embarrassed that I practically nuzzled into him like a damn cat, but Xander means safety. His warmth soaked into me, as did his whiskey and cigar scent. Xander meant home now. I remember him carrying me out and to the car, then nothing.

I must have passed out from the adrenaline because now that I think about it, I feel something soft underneath me. It's not exactly soft enough to be my bed, but maybe a couch. Realization hits and I focus more on my surroundings. I can smell my guys, Xander's whiskey and cigar, Maverick's fresh cotton and rain, and Jax's gunpowder and aftershave. All my favorite smells. I focus on the sounds next, the click-clack of typing, the soft steps of someone pacing and the ticktock of a wall clock.

"I think I have something." Xander's deep voice almost startles me. "I've been going over Adrian's father's dealing with us and everything else I could find. It seems he had a few real estate properties around town. It might be worth checking them out."

"What do you think we might find?" Maverick asks. His voice is coming and going, so he must be the one pacing.

"I don't know, but something that leads us to that prick. If we're lucky, Adrian himself." I hear some shuffling of feet before Xander speaks again. "Take some extra men and Jax. If you find him, keep him alive."

I hear a deep chuckle come from Jax, but worry shoots through me, causing me to snap up to sit. "Wait."

"Princess. I knew you weren't asleep." A second later, Jax scoops me up into his arms and holds me tight. "Don't worry, baby. You're safe here. Me and Mav will be back soon, I promise." Wrapping my arms around his thick neck, I squeeze. I know my men can take care of themselves, but Adrian is ruthless and doesn't fight fair.

"Be safe. Come home to me, please." Finding his face with my hands, I lean in for a kiss. This kiss is gentle, tender-like, trying to tell him everything I feel with no words.

"I will, Princess." He pulls away a second later, the cold of the room creeping in before it's replaced by another warm body. Maverick. His fresh scent of cotton and rain fills my senses. Reminding me of cozying up with a good book by a window during a rainstorm.

"Don't worry Angel. I'll keep the big ape out of trouble." Maverick holds me like he never wants to let go before leaning down and kissing my forehead. "Promise me you'll keep the boss man out of trouble as well." I try to hold back my giggle, but it escapes anyway. "Music to my ears." This time, I blush at his words.

"Take care of each other. I need both of you to come home in one piece." As much as I don't want to let go yet, I release my grip on his shirt and take a small step back.

"Take care of our girl, Xander." Jax calls out, sounding further away. I stand there, unsure of where I am or who else is around, as two sets of footsteps lead away from me.

My mind wonders when a set of hands grabs my shoulders. My body reacts as I jerk back.

"Little bird, it's just me." I force my racing heart to calm. "We're in my office downtown." He pulls me into his embrace and I instantly relax. "They're going to be okay, baby. Come sit with me." He reaches down and wraps his arms around mine before leading me away from what I'm assuming is a couch. Reaching out with my unclaimed hand, I feel my surroundings. My hand hits something hard a moment later, which I'm guessing is a wooden desk. I trace my fingers along the edge as Xander leads me around and takes a seat, pulling me down onto his lap. I lean back into his chest as his hands rest on my thighs. Slowly, he draws light circles with his fingers on my bare skin, sending tingles up my legs. The exhaustion of today's events hit me like a brick wall.

"Little Bird, we need to know what Adrian said to you earlier." My body tenses at his words. I don't want to relive it again. Not yet, at least.

When I keep my mouth shut, Xander slowly glides his hand up my thigh, over my dress, up my stomach until he reaches my throat. Ever so slowly, as if waiting for me to protest, his large hand wraps around my neck in a loose but firm hold. His thumb moves up and down as he leans forward to whisper into my ear. "Do you need me to get your mind off today, Little Bird?" Swallowing, I give him a few nods of my head. "You know better than that. Use your words, Wren."

Taking a deep breath, I press my ass into the thick bulge growing beneath me. "Yes, please." I can feel how wet my core is getting, and Xander only makes it worse by grinding up into my ass. My sensitive nipples pebble, scraping against the lacey fabric of my bralette. The other hand, Xander has on my thigh, glides up my leg in a slow, agonizing pace as he keeps hold of my movements with the hands still firmly wrapped around my small throat. My body twitches in anticipation when his fingers glide against my panty covered core. A moan escapes my throat as Xander thrusts his hips up once more.

"I know what you need, baby. Let me take care of you." His lips softly graze my ear, sending pleasurable goosebumps down my entire body as his hand between my legs grips the fabric of my panties. "Let me worship you, Little Bird." The moment those words leave his lips, he tugs. The sound of fabric ripping sounds before a sting of pain hits. In the next second, Xander's fingers swept over my core, teasing me with his touch.

My back arches off Xander's chest as my need for this man's touch turns feral. These men can turn me into a puddle of want and so much more with a simple flick of their fingers. Letting out another needy moan, Xander finally takes pity on me and gives me what my body is craving. His fingers run up through my folds before gliding down to my core. "So wet for me, Little Bird. So needy. You're soaking wet, just for me to enjoy." My pussy spasms around the tip of Xander's finger that's teasing my opening. Ever so slowly, he presses his digit into my core. Before I know it, he is pulling out and replacing one with two, then three, but I need more. He starts to fuck me with his fingers at a steady pace, in, out, in, out. Curling them just right to make my toes curl.

"P-please Xander." My words are a plea to stop teasing and to just fuck me. The hand around my throat loosens its hold before shifting down to my chest. My dress has a sweetheart line, so the top of my breast peek out. The thin straps that band around my shoulders had no chance against this man as he grips the fabric at my breast and yanks. The top half of my dress falls to my waist as Xander's hand replaces the material. His thumb and forefinger pinching and tugging at my pebbled nipple.

"Look at these pretty pink nipples. I bet that pussy of yours is just as pretty right now. Should I find out?" I nod my head as I press my chest further into his rough hands. He lets out a chuckle at my over eagerness. Suddenly, his hands leave my body, and I almost cry out in protest before he shifts, rising from his seated position. I move with him to stand, thinking we are going to move to the couch, but he grabs my wrists and moves them to the desk in front of us. His foot taps at mine to open up my legs, and I do as he demands. "Now be a good girl and stay just like this." I do as I'm told and listen to the rustling of fabric behind me.

I should be embarrassed. Standing half naked, bent over a desk, no underwear, and the top of my dress hanging around my waist, but I'm not.

"Don't move Baby." Hands glide up my legs a second later and I have to force myself not to jump at the contact. When he reaches my upper thighs, my dress gets flipped up over my ass before Xander shoves his face between my thighs. His tongue instantly making contact with my core, and I moan at the feeling. I needed this after everything today. Xander's hands wrap around my thighs and yanks them apart and back, shoving himself deeper as he devours me like a man starved. He lets out a groan of his own as his once eager licks slow before stopping all together.

"I need you, Wren. I need to fuck you, fill you full of my cum. I want you dripping with me when the others come home tonight. Can you handle that, Little Bird?" I nod eagerly for him to do just that. I'm so drunk on lust, I forget Xander's rule. A second later, Xander is molded to my back, his hand wrapped around my throat, and pulling back as he places his lips next to my ear. "Words."

It takes everything in me to speak, but I do. "Y-Yes. I want that." Xander places a soft kiss on my pulse point before lining his hips up with mine. I can feel his cock slide against my wet core and my pussy cries out with excitement. He thrusts his thick cock against my core a few times in a teasing manner before adjusting himself, the tip right at my core. "Please Xander." I'm begging at this point.

"Wren. I love you." The words penetrate the lusty fog a half second before Xander slams home. I feel a pinch of pain from the stretch of Xander's size, but he gives me a second to breathe before he moves again. I don't have a chance to process Xander's words before he moves. He starts with a slow but steady pace, in and out. His firm hand is around my throat, keeping me still as he pounds into me. My hips bump the hard edge of the desk as my hands slip against the slick wood. My orgasm builds with each thrust of Xander's hips, his cock hitting a certain spot just right that causes mini shocks to shoot through my core. "Fuck. Fuck. Fuck. Wrennnn... Fuck." Xander's slow pace breaks as he starts to pistol his hips against my ass. Our combined moans and the slapping of skin, an orchestra of sounds. I'm on the edge of total bliss when Xander leans down, forcing my head to turn in his direction, and takes my mouth with his. His thrusts barely falter as he devours me, body and soul. My climax hits me like a hurricane, my body sparking to life with pure euphoria. Xander must follow me over the edge as he thrusts once more before settling deep within. Our breathing is erratic as we try to catch our breaths. My pulse going a mile a minute before skipping a beat at Xander's next whispered words.

"I love you, Wren, and I will kill anyone who thinks they can hurt you."

Chapter Fifteen

Jaxon

Adrian's father had over twenty owned properties around the city. Most seem to be empty apartments or storefronts. I'm guessing some were safe houses and others pit stops for shipments. The late Mr. West was a businessman to the core. Anything he could get his dirty hands on to make a little cash, he would. Drugs, weapons, skins — he didn't care. He wasn't a horrible man, but money can really change a man. Just like his entitled little asshat of a son. My guess is: He is still hiding behind daddy, even after the man is dead and buried.

Mav and I, along with about six other men in a separate car, head to the first address on the south side of the city. We didn't want to leave Wren, not with her clinging to me like she feared for my life. I've never had anyone care for me like Wren does. The guys always cared, but it's different when it's a woman. Your woman, but I know Xander will keep her safe. Plus, we all know Wren will be the safest once we catch this bastard.

Pulling up to our destination, we take all the precautions, parking a few houses down before heading to the back of our SUV. Waiting for the others to join us, Mav and I grab two 9mms a piece, plus some extra ammo. We each tuck away one for backup. This isn't our first rodeo, so having a spare could save your life.

Once we all grouped up, we head for the house, keeping to the shadows. The sun fell about half an hour ago, so the brisk night helps to hide us. We split up into two teams. The first, Mav and I, with two other men, take positions at the front of the house, while the other four head to the back. Once the signal is given, two sharp whistles, we move as one. I kick in the front door, and we go in, guns blazing. Not willing to take any more chances to let Adrian get the upper hand. Room by room, we clean the place within seconds. Empty. There are signs that someone might have been here before, but it could have been anyone at any time. Even squatters.

"Motherfucker!" Mav yells, kicking the wall. "This is going to take all night and we don't even know if he's going to be in one of these addresses."

"He can't run forever. So, let's leave him a message." Looking around the place, I notice it's pretty bare. Idea after idea drifts through my mind, but only one sparks some joy. Turning to one of our men, I give him my orders. "Run back to the SUV and grab a spare gas can." He gives me a nod before heading out. Turning back to Maverick, I give him my best grin. "Let's burn his shit to the ground." The savage grin on Mav returns tells me everything.

After setting fire to the first address, we move on. Addresses number two through seven are busts as well. Each one looking like the first. Bare and empty of any actual sign of Adrian. But with fires going up around the city, we're betting Adrian has either already gotten the message that we are hunting him, or he will soon.

Address eight is a bit more promising. The empty storefront looked less deserted. A couple of blankets, take out boxes, etc. What made us believe it was used by Adrian was the computer setup. A laptop and extra monitor sat in the far corner on a plain metal desk. We collected the laptop for one of the tech guys and burned the rest to the ground.

It's been two hours since we started and every address was a bust, but with one left, we powered on. All we want to do is head home to our girl. The last place is a small three-bedroom house on the east side of the city. It's also the closest to our home. "Let's get this over with. I smell like gasoline and need a shower." Mav calls out as we wait for the other six men to join us again. I give him a quick nod before cracking my neck and stretching my arms out.

I have a feeling about this one address. It's not a good one. Would Adrian be that dumb to set up base this close to our home? Possibly risk being seen. The answer is yes. He seems stupid enough and eager enough to get his hands on Wren to pull a cocky move like that.

In no time, we are all in position, ready to end the night when I give the signal. This time, Mav kicks in the back door and we all charge in. Guns raised and at the ready. We enter through the kitchen and split in different directions to clear the house. Lowering my gun, I holster when I find nothing in the living room. Thinking we hit another fucking brick wall of nothing, I pull out my phone and dial Xander but right as he answers I hear Mav call out to me from the back of the house.

I can hear Xander asking me a question on the other side of the phone. "Did you find anything?" I'm about to reply when I enter the doorway of the room Maverick is in. My jaw hits the floor a second before my shock wears off.

"That motherfucking asshole. I'm going to string him up by his intestines. Cut off his dick and make him choke on it. Fuck him up the ass with a baseball bat full of screws." Every possible way to kill a man in the worst, most painful way pops into my head faster than I can spit them out. I'm so lost in my rage that I don't even realize the hand with my phone in it is going through a wall. When I pull it back out, drywall dust flies everywhere and my phone is smashed. Fuck.

Maverick's phone rings a second later. He answers and places it on speaker. How Mav is staying calm is a surprise to me, especially after seeing all this shit. "Someone tell me what the fuck is going on?"

I leave Mav to explain it all as I move closer to the wall. My eyes shift all over the place, trying to sort out everything I see. "Well, the best way to explain it is some type of stalkers shrine of Wren. Hundreds of pictures of Wren are all over the wall. Some of her and Abby at her bookshop. Some of her and one of us, but our faces are blacked out. If I took a guess, Adrian is more than obsessed with Wren, man." Faintly, I hear Xander let out his own curse, but I'm too focused on this wall of my Princess. She looks gorgeous in all the photos, but the fact Adrian had them taken enrages me to no ends.

"Pack it all up and bring it back. Wren is worried and wants you guys home soon." With no further words needed, he hangs up.

Mav steps up next to me as I focus on the images more closely. "These are all from the last two weeks. How has no one noticed someone following us?"

"I don't know, man, but I'm betting he had someone else take these. He knows we are looking for him and would easily notice him, but you heard Xander. Our woman is waiting for us. Let's pack it up and burn it down." He slaps me on the back and barks orders at the men to take everything down. Within minutes, the house is cleared and a trail of gasoline leads out to the front porch. "Would you like to do the honors, brother?" Maverick hands me a lighter, making me grin.

"With pleasure." Leaning down, I light the lighter and place the small yet mighty flame on the trail of accelerant. With a whoosh, the gasoline lights, rushing to the house. We stand there for a few minutes, wanting to make sure it all burns.

I watch the flames dance in the late-night sky a few seconds longer than the others. Forcing myself to turn away, I whisper a promise to the wind. "Run and hide, Adrian, but your time is almost up."

It doesn't take long to get back to the house. I've been working on calming my anger since we left the last address, but nothing is helping. All I can see is the wall of hundreds of pictures of Wren. Someone was able to get close enough to take them without one of us noticing. Which is honestly just another kick to the dick. How could we let that happen? Let Adrian play this little cat-and-mouse game with us. And why the fuck haven't we caught this fucker yet?

I'm still loathing in my own self-hatred when Mav pulls to a stop in front of the house. Glancing out the window, I spot the light on in the den. Meaning Wren is probably there waiting for us. A part of me wants to rip open the door and run to her like something out of an old romance movie, but I force myself to not move.

A hand slapping my chest has me snapping a glare over to Mav in the driver's seat. "Look, Jax. I know, seeing that wall was... well, overwhelming, but you're not the only one beating themselves up because of it. We underestimated that prick, but I think tonight's message was loud and clear." He lets out a heavy exhale as if the world was on his shoulder. "Wren is in there waiting for us. She may not be able to see your grumpy ass look, but I bet you a hundred bucks she will sense it. So you need to get over whatever is making you this way, and fast. There is way too much going on to be stressing Wren out more with your PMSing attitude." I shake my head at him. He just doesn't understand. I'm the unofficial official enforcer. It's my job to keep an eye out and protect my family, and I missed someone following Wren. "Jax, I love you, man. You're my brother, but I'm not afraid to beat your ass if you upset my angel. Now grow a fucking pair and get your ass inside. Our woman is waiting." He doesn't wait for my reply this time, simply exits the SUV and heads for the front door. I can see the men from tonight are unloading all the evidence and taking it in through the garage. Smart. Wren doesn't need to hear some of the things we found.

I think what pissed me off the most about the wall were the pictures not from the past two weeks. Pictures of when Wren could see and her bright blues were full of life. Those are the ones that got under my skin. Images of her half naked and tied to a bed, looking like she just wanted to disappear. I think the sick fuck wanted us to find this place. To play with our heads.

Deciding that Mav is right, I drag my ass out of the SUV and up the steps to the front door. Taking a deep breath, I roll my shoulders and try to release all my built-up anger. Wren deserves better, and Mav is also right about her and her sixth sense. She's always been able to sense moods and I don't need her to feel like I'm upset with her when really it's me.

I'm about to turn the knob of the handle when the front door flies open and there in the doorway stands Wren. She stares blankly at me, but it penetrates my soul all the same. "Princess." The moment the nickname leaves my lips, she rushes me. Throwing herself into my arms, and like she was always meant to be there, my hands reach under her ass and lift. Her thighs instantly take their place around my waist, as her arms band around my neck and her face nuzzles my jaw line. This is home. This time, when I inhale, I try to breathe in Wren. Her scent of fresh flowers and old books is a balm to my heart. Even when she doesn't go to the bookshop, her scent of books and ink is present and so unique to Wren.

"What took you so long to come in?" Her voice is muffled, with her face still tucked into my neck. I spy Xander and Mav at the corner of the entry of the den. That attention stealing mutt sitting at their feet with what I can only describe as a glare point in my direction. Xander raises a brow in my direction before shaking his head and heading back into the den. Mav just shakes his head like I'm an idiot and follows after. Ares continues to watch me as I carry Wren back to the den, still wrapped in my arms tight. It's like she knows I need this, her touch, her warmth.

I make my way to the couch and take a seat, letting Wren get more comfortable in my lap. The mutt, Ares, finds that it's the perfect opportunity to jump up and make himself comfortable as well, with his head in my woman's lap. Xander glares at the dog, while Maverick smirks. I make eye contact with both men sitting across from us. Xander lets out a sigh before nodding. We don't want to tell her about anything we found tonight, but we also don't want to hide anything either.

Wren rests her head against my chest, giving me her strength. "Wren, at first, we didn't want to tell you, but we think you have the right to know." From the corner of my eye, I can see Wren frowning.

"Know what?" I look up at the guys one more time to make sure this is the right move.

"When we left the office earlier, it was with information that Adrian's father had a list of real estate properties still under the family name. We thought Adrian might use one to hide out at. We didn't find much in any of them. Only a laptop, until the last one." Wren hasn't moved a muscle since I started talking. I'm almost afraid she isn't breathing, but I need to get it all out. She needs to know Adrian is a bigger threat, and that she needs to be protected. "The last house was only ten minutes from here. One room was set up as some type of shrine to you. Photos of you were all over the wall. New ones but also older ones." Her body goes stiff at that.

"We've sent Adrian a clear message tonight. It should actually be on the news now." Mav calls out, reaching for the TV remote and flipping channels until he lands on the news. Turning up the volume, the news anchor's voice sounds through the room.

"Devastating fires broke out throughout our city tonight as firefighters rush to put them out. So far, there doesn't seem to be any injured parties, but the fire chief will be looking into the cases as being arson. If you, or anyone you might know, have any information, please contact our tip line. For now, that's all the information we have, but stay tuned for updates as they come." The woman continues to talk, moving on to a new story, but Mav turns it down, a wicked and proud smile painting his face.

"Y-you burned down houses?" Wren asks, sounding concerned.

"Yes. And a few storefronts. No one was in them when they were started, if that's what you're concerned about." Xander's tone is casual, like he would have burned them down with Adrian's people in them too if we could. He isn't wrong, either. I'll kill anyone who gets in our way to getting that asshole, Adrian.

"So now what?" Wren asks, adjusting herself so that she can semi-face the others, but that's the million-dollar question.

What is Adrian West's next move?

Chapter Sixteen

Maverick

I know we all agreed not to hide everything from Wren because she has a right to know about Adrian. He is the one stalking her now, but we all agreed that Wren shouldn't know what we plan to do to that prick once he's in our grip. Telling my little angel that we burned down Adrian's property today should have scared her. I expected to see horror or disgust towards us, but once she realized it didn't actually harm anyone, she seemed less shocked.

I watch Wren closely as she turns in Jax's lap so that she can focus more on all of us. That's the thing about this woman. She understands people. It's like she can already tell what we need, her attention. It's hard sharing one woman, but Wren doesn't single any of us out. She tries to give us all our own time and attention and knows when one of us might need it more.

My Angel frowns as she reaches over and runs her fingers through Ares fur. She gives him a few scratches behind the ears and the dog melts further into her lap. That dog was the best purchase I have ever made. Since the moment they met, Ares hasn't left her side. He follows her around like he thinks she hung the moon. I would be jealous if I wasn't so secure in mine and her relationship now.

Her previous question still hangs in the air. None of us are sure of what to tell her. Honestly, I think we all know what now. We wait for Adrian's next move. Tonight, we made a statement, a declaration, or war, really. Glancing back up at the television, I see the channel flashing back to a sky view of the city. Yellow and orange lit the skyline. The small fires are still lighting the night sky due to not enough manpower in the city to put them all out. It's almost poetic in a twisted way. You attempt to take something from us, and we will take something from you.

After a few minutes of silence, Wren speaks again. "I don't understand. Why does Adrian want me? Why now?" Her voice fluctuates with her emotions. She's trying to stay strong for us. For herself, but with each day that bastard is free, the risk gets greater. I'm guessing he is planning something and buying time, but for what?

"My guess is it has to do with us," Xander says, taking another sip of his whiskey. His eyes are trained on Wren, like always whenever she is in the room. Ever since that first night, he was obsessed. I never understood why until I actually met her. She is all that is good in this world, unlike us, sinners since a young age. Wren might have had a rough go for a while, but you would have never guessed it by looking at her. She didn't let that piece of shit destroy her completely.

"What do you mean?" This question makes us all chuckle. It's obvious to us now.

"He wants what he can't have. In his mind, when you were with him, he owned you. You were his. He thought you were dead, but now he knows you're not. His twisted mind thinks you still are his even if he wanted you dead at one point and now, he wants you back. Seeing you with other men, men who he hates, makes it worse. I believe he will stop at nothing to have you, and if he can't have you..." Xander pauses before looking over at me next to him, then Jax on the couch, then back to Wren in his lap. "Then no one can," Wren gasps. Her white eyes going wide at the realization.

"So, he's going to go after you guys as well?" Ares nuzzles Wren's thigh, sensing her stress and worry and comforting her. "No." She shakes her head. "No. I won't let him hurt anyone else because of me." We all know where her thoughts are going, and I can't have that.

"Don't you dare even suggest what you are thinking, Angel. We are grown ass men and can handle ourselves. If you think sacrificing yourself for us is the only way, you have another thing coming. Who's to say that once he has you, he wouldn't use you to bring us down, anyway?" I'm on the edge of my seat now, furious that she would even think of doing something like that for us.

Slowly, Wren climbs off Jax's lap, making the beast of a man glare at me as she crosses the small distance to me. Moving to kneel in front of me, she reaches her hands up and gently cups my face. My entire demeanor relaxes at her touch. Soft and warm.

"I'm sorry, Mav. My intention was not to upset you. I- I'm just so afraid of something happening to you three. Not only that, but I just found you all and now someone is trying to take me away from you. Even though it hasn't been long and the four of us being in a relationship is still new, I couldn't bear the thought of him taking one of you away from me." I've never had anyone care for me like Wren cares for us. It's always been fake and dependent on what I could provide for them. Wren suddenly stands, causing Ares to jump off the couch and stand next to her.

She twines her fingers through his fur before turning and facing our direction.

It's obvious she has a statement to make, so we keep quiet and let her do her thing. Each of us is still glancing at each other, not sure what to expect and honestly, it's nerve wracking. Wren standing there in a light baby blue nightgown and matching fuzzy slippers. Her nipples are peaked and showing through the thin, silky material. All her creamy white skin is on display for our eyes. This woman is beyond striking, and she's not even trying to be sexy for us. My cock hardens at the thought of the things I wish I could do to her right now, but I have to force myself to focus. This is serious. Wren wants to tell us something.

The woman in question takes a deep inhale before slowly releasing it. "Look. I still have no idea how the four of us are supposed to work. I mean, honestly, how the hell is one woman supposed to keep three men satisfied? It's crazy, really, but I also don't think I can bear sharing you with anyone. Especially not now, not when feelings have changed." Another deep breath. "I've been so nervous to say it because I've been afraid that it's not true, but it's not fair that I've told Jax and not Mav and Xander." Glancing over at Jax, the asshole puffs out his chest, a satisfied smirk on his ugly face. "But you all have shown your feelings to me in different ways. Mav, you got me Ares, and it was the best gift. When you three aren't around, I feel safe with him. Xander, I know you're the one who brings me all the stacks of books in my room. Jax, you've been a giant teddy bear, always knowing when I just need a hug. There is so much more, like when you guys took care of my shop after kidnapping me. Then letting Abby have a job and allowing me..." The woman is spiraling, standing there twisting her fingers through Ares' fur. Luckily, Xander steps in to regain her focus.

"Little Bird. What is the rule?" The three of us smirk at that as Wren snaps her mouth shut and nibbles on her bottom lip.

"What I've been trying to say is that... I love you. All of you. Each of you has told me, but I need you all to know that I love you back. I don't know what the future holds for us, but in case we don't get much time, I want you all to know that." The smile that lights my face would be blinding. She was doing well until the last part. In case, we don't get much time. Over my dead body, will we not grow old together.

Xander abruptly stands and steps in front of Wren, pinching her chin and forcing her to look up at him. "Say it again," he demands.

"I love you." Wren's words are soft yet strong. And before Wren knows it, Xander is slamming his lips down on hers. The chub from early had just barely gone away, but now it's back as Xander wraps his arms under Wren's ass and lifts. He pulls away for half a second, looking down at Ares, then me before nodding to the door. His "get the mutt out of here", was read loud and clear as he turns to Jax. Looking down at Ares, I nod my head to the door and, like he knows it's about to get X-rated, trots off.

When I turn around from closing the door; because we don't need to kill any house staff for walking in at the wrong time. I see Wren leaning back against Jax's chest, her nightgown around her hips, and Xander's head between her thighs. And just like that, I'm rock fucking hard.

I take my seat across from the show, adjust my chair, so I can have a front-row view. Wren's moans fill the small den as Xander eats her like a man starved, while Jax pinches and tweaks her nipples. Fuck, that is one of the hottest things I've ever seen. After a few minutes, I have to adjust my dick in my pants. I'm so hard that I'm pretty sure my dick has a zipper imprint now.

Wren's pleas fill the silence next. "More. I need more. Please." Xander pulls away before sitting back on his heels and nods me over.

"You heard our woman. She needs more." I give him a smirk before scooping up Wren. I place her back to my chest and hold her thighs open before presenting her glistening wet pussy to Xander again. The man wastes no time diving back between her juicy thighs as she tilts her head up, and I take her mouth in mine. I can hear the rustle of clothes as Jax undresses behind us, as Wren's all too willing body gets lost in lust.

From the corner of my eye, I can see Jax, legs spread and hand pumping his cock as he watches Wren. A second later, Wren's body tenses, her toes curl, and her back arches off my chest. Xander doubles his efforts, working her core with his tongue, before the sound of Wren's melodious cry of release echoes off the rooms.

"We're not done with you, Little Bird." Xander stands and captures Wren's lips, making her taste herself on him before grabbing her thighs and turning her to Jax. He lowers her down slowly, Jax helping guide her over his cock. The moment his tip enters, Wren all but melts back into Jax.

"So full. So good." Wren's husky voice does something to me as I watch Jax slowly lift her before letting gravity do the work and slam her back-down on his cock. Jax's groans of pleasure mix with Wren's moans as I take my seat again. This time getting more comfortable and losing my clothes. Sitting there in all my tan and naked glory, I slowly stroke myself as Xander gets undressed and moves into position.

He climbs onto the couch, lifting one leg and placing it on the back to steady himself.

"Wren, tell us again." He demands, pumping his own dick inches away from Wren's face.

"I!" thrust "Love!" thrust "You!" thrust "All!"

"Good girl. Now open up and tell me again." Like the good girl Xander just called her, she does just that. His hand is replaced by her pretty little tongue as he glides his dick over it, soaking him before sliding further into her mouth.

As one, the three of them move, Jax thrusting up, Xander pumping his hips, sending his cock further down Wren's throat. It's like art. The groans and moans that fill the room are a symphony of sounds, and I have to force myself to not come like some teenage boy watching porn in his room. I slow my movements and they speed up. Xander curses a second before one last thrust and I get to watch as our woman, as she swallows every last drop before licking her lips clean as he pulls away. Jax lasts only a few moments longer.

"Fuck, that's it baby, squeeze me. Milk me for everything I have. Fuckkkkkk, Wren." One finally thrust and Jax is down for the count. I grin to myself as I stand. My turn.

"Fuck, that was hot, Angel, but I hope you didn't forget about me." The little minx shakes her head, giving me a devilish grin in return.

"I would never." Tilting her head back, she finds Jax's lips, and she whispers, "I love you, Big Guy." Then kisses him before shifting to climb off. Standing, she glances toward Xander, steps up to him, and gives him a kiss as well. "I love you, Xander." This kiss is more Xander telling her he loves her too before he leaves her gasping for air.

Xander and Jax take up positions on the couch, not bothering to dress, but I don't care as my focus switches to the woman in front of me. She's still wearing her baby blue nightgown around her waist, so I wiggle it down over her hips before skimming my nose back up her belly and to her throat. With no warning, I yank her flush to me. She let out a small squeak before giggling as I lift her and move us back to the chair I was watching from. My cock sits between Wren's plump cheeks as I take my seat. Her breasts are pushed against my chest, her pebbled nipples hard against my skin as she raises her hip, my dick springing up to meet her dripping core before she slowly lowers herself. I stare at her, trying to memorize every wrinkle, freckle, and scar she has on her face. The woman has always been breathtaking, but right now is something else. Naked, bear, and vulnerable to us.

"I love you, Maverick." Fuckkkkkk... I've had women tell me they loved me before, but it's never felt like this. Like the entire world just froze, and my heart skipped a beat.

"I love you more than the air I breathe, Angel." The words aren't even a thought as they leave my lips, but the moment they do, I know it's the truth.

It's like there is no more that needs to be said as Wren takes charge. She grinds her hips back and forth. The feel of her pussy wrapped around my cock is pure ecstasy as she rides me. Glancing over her shoulder, I see the other two pumping their cocks again. Ha. I know exactly what watching Wren does to a man. Focusing back on my naked woman riding me, I lean forward and nip at her nipple before sucking it into my mouth. My hands on her hips grind her harder as she picks up speed, this time chasing her own euphoria. My climax climbs as Wren fucks herself on my cock, head thrown back, pressing her breasts further into my mouth. Her pussy tightens, and I can't hold back any longer. Wren cums, the sound of her moan, sending me over the edge next. Her tight pussy milks my cock in tightening aftershocks as I release everything I have into her.

A sick and twisted part of me hopes one of us gets Wren pregnant soon. An image of her belly big and round, miniature versions of us running around the house. Wren would make an amazing mother and among the three of us, I think we could make at least one decent father. Thinking of us as fathers has me glance back at the others, who are now wiping themselves up with whatever discarded clothes they could find.

Wren leans forward and rests her head on my chest, eyes fluttering close. My cock slips out of her as Jax steps up and gently cleans between her legs. I shift her to the side, cradling her in my arms as I stand. "Alright, Angel. Let's get you to bed."

She lets out a big yawn before whispering once more. "I love you guys." Seconds later, Wren's fast asleep. Turning, I head for the door to take her upstairs, so I can tuck her in when I hear Jax.

"I will never get tired of her telling us that."

Same brother, same.

Chapter Seventeen

Wren

My dream world fades as I slowly wake up. I stretch out my arms and legs and groan at the delightful ache I feel between my thighs. Last night plays around in my head on repeat. I was so nervous about telling the guys I love them. It sounds ridiculous since I've already told one of them, but telling them all how I really feel, just felt even more real. What if I told them and this was all a joke? Or a week or two from now, they will get tired of me? But I had to pull up my big girl panties and tell them because tomorrow is never promised. Plus, the way they touched me last night told me more than they needed to say. They have always been pretty good at expressing themselves through my body, and my body doesn't mind at all.

I reach to the side of me, expecting to feel a warm body, but all I feel is cool sheets. I frown at that because one of my men is always still in bed with me until I wake up. Listening for movement in the bathroom or down the hall, I hear nothing. My frown deepens as I push myself to a sitting position. My feet hover over the carpeted floor for a second until I scoot further to the edge. I almost jumped out of my skin when, instead of the soft plush carpet, my feet hit rough fur. I nearly tumbled off the bed but caught myself at the last second. Ares pops up and starts rubbing his body against my legs, making me giggle.

"Ares, you almost gave me a heart attack. Next time, just climb in bed with me if they leave." Once again, proving how smart he is, Ares jumps up on the bed and makes himself comfortable. I shake my head at the silly dog. I swear he understands everything I say.

I shuffle my feet into the fuzzy slippers on the floor. Someone always leaves me a pair in the morning. My guess is Jax, but there's no telling with these men sometimes. Standing, I take a step toward the bedroom door when the overwhelming urge to vomit hits again. My hand rushes to cover my mouth as I make an immediate U-turn and head for the bathroom instead. The bathroom door slams open with a push, but I barely flinch at the loud sound before I'm rushing to my knee and throwing up. It's not surprising that barely anything comes up since it's early morning and I haven't eaten since dinner last night, but my stomach continues to contract. The painful waves of nausea last for about five minutes before I realize, I'm not alone. Fuck.

"Wren, we're going to the hospital." Xander demands as I slump back against the bathtub after wiping my mouth and flushing.

"Xander, I'm fine. It's a stomach bug. That's all. I'm sure you've been sick before." The click-clack of nails sounds a second before Ares' big fluffy head drops into my lap.

"Ares! Get off of her." Xander's tone is serious, making me roll my eyes. Not that he notices.

"Don't yell at him. He's just doing his job and trying to make me feel better. Now, can you help me up?" Xander wraps his large hand around my biceps before pulling me to my feet. Ares lets out a huff before pressing his body against my legs for support.

"Wren. You've been throwing up off and on for over the last two weeks. I don't think it's just a stomach bug. What if something serious like a stomach problem? I'm not a doctor and neither are you, so you can't just keep saying it's a stomach bug." I let out a deep breath as he leads me back into the bedroom. Is it possible to love and hate how overprotective someone is of you?

"Can I think about it? I have a lot to do at the shop today and honestly, I feel better already. I'll get dressed and meet you downstairs in a few minutes." He pauses us by the bed, so I turn into his body, lift up on my tiptoes, reach for his face and land a big ole kiss on his lips. "I know you care, but I promise you I'm fine. I would tell you if I thought it was something serious. So please give me a few minutes to think about it. Also, could you pretty please ask Marie to make those banana chocolate chip pancakes? Those sound so good right now." Xander lets out an inaudible sigh before grabbing my cheeks and kissing me with passion back.

"Tell me again."

"I love you Xander."

"I love you too, Little Bird. You have ten minutes." A quick smack to my ass and he's gone. The quiet click of the door closing is all I hear before I'm alone with my thoughts.

After a minute of really thinking about it, I decide Xander might have a point. The only symptom I have is the random nausea and rushing to the bathroom to puke. No fever, chills, cough, runny nose.

LOVE IS BLIND

Quickly dressing in whatever outfit Abby left out for me, I slip on my tennis shoes. The outfit feels casual, soft leggings and a baggy t-shirt. Once again, I thank whichever gods sent this woman to me because I swear some days, she just knows what I need and after yesterday's events, and excitement, I really just need a laid-back day.

"Alright Ares, you ready to face the wolves? I have a feeling the guys are going to want me to stay home again." Another doggy huff and we are out.

We make our way down the stairs. Ares's pressed close as we descend. The smell of sweet treats cooking fills my senses as I make my way to the kitchen. I'm practically drooling at the thought of these pancakes. I speed up just a bit in my excitement and realize it was the wrong move as I stumble over my own feet, sending myself flying forwards. There's nothing I can do but brace for impact until arms wrap around me and pull me up to hit a hard chest instead of the hard wall or floor I was aiming for.

"Woah there, Princess. What's the hurry?" Jax's deep voice fills my ears, and I blush before answering.

"Pancakes?" I say shyly, making him chuckle.

"I see, and here I thought you might be excited to see me." My blush darkens.

"I mean, I am, but pancakes are life." This time I say the words with all the seriousness I can muster, which isn't much. Jax lets out a really deep laugh this time before kissing the top of my head.

"Fair enough. Well, let's get you there in one piece, then." I grin up at him as he leads me the rest of the way into the kitchen and to the breakfast nook I like to sit at. Other voices follow in after us and I hear the tail end of the conversations.

"...go to the hospital, and she should also stay home until we get the bastard." This is said from Xander, which makes me scowl. He would be the one who wants me to stay home. I understand his concern and I have my own concerns about leaving the house, but staying hidden only proves to Adrian, he wins. He wants me to be scared of my own shadow. Metaphorically now.

"I understand, but she should get a choice t-." Maverick's words cut off, probably because he noticed me, but I liked the things he was saying.

"Please continue." I say, waiting patiently for my food and also trying not to yell at them for talking about my life behind my back again.

"Wren, we are worried about you, that's all." Maverick continues coming up to me and kissing the top of my head.

My shoulders slump a little. Me being defensive won't solve anything, plus I've already decided to get checked out.

Letting out a huff, I tell them just that. "Fine. I'll go see Doc. I trust him, but you all can't come." A chorus of what's, and no's sound before the click of a plate being set down in front of me catches my attention. "Thank you, Marie, you're the best." Feeling around the counter, I find my fork and quickly dig in. The first bit is heavenly as the chocolate and banana melts in my mouth.

"Little Bird, someone needs to go with you." Xander exclaims, and I smile wide as I hear just the person I was thinking about entering the room.

"Are those banana chocolate chip pancakes? Yumm." Abby's sunshine filled voice sounds and I look in her direction.

"Abby can go with me, and after, I plan to go to work." I hold up a hold to stop any rebuts. "No, if and or buts about it. You can wait outside the appointment or meet us at the shop, but I'm going." I aggressively shove another bite of pancake in my mouth, proving how serious I am.

Before any more arguing can be done, cell phones go off around the room. I hear at least three, so I'm guessing it's my men's. I frown as all three answer their phones. All three talk at the same time, making it hard to understand any one conversation, but I get snippets. Fire. Warehouse. Sighting.

After another minute, the conversations go quiet. "What's wrong? What happened?" I call out. They are probably having a staring conversation with each other, but I'm not stupid. I know this has something to do with Adrian.

"Wren, we have to go. It seems we didn't have to wait long for that asshole to retaliate. We will explain more later. I'll call Doc and let him know you're on your way. Jax, get a few extra men to escort the women to Doc and her shop." I'm suddenly spun around in my chair, and I am facing a hard chest. "Little Bird, listen closely. You are to go straight to Doc's to get checked out. Call us with what he says. Then straight to the shop, no leaving. Listen to my men. One of us will pick you up at the shop as soon as we can. Okay?" Worry races through my body, but I force myself not to show it. Whatever is going on, they don't need to worry about me. They need to focus.

"Okay. Doc's, the shop, then wait for you." I repeat, knowing Xander needs me to tell him I understand the plan. "If anything happens, listen to our men." I add, so he knows I'll do just that.

"We will see you soon, Little Bird. I love you." Xander kisses me fiercely before he steps away, and Jax steps up.

"Be good Princess." His kiss is demanding, but filled with so much need. "Love you, baby." Then he too is gone before my final lover steps up.

"Angel, use your sixth sense. If you feel like something is off, call us." I give him a small nod. "I love you, Angel." Maverick's kiss is soft and gentle and leaves me wanting more, and he pulls away as well. "Abby, keep an eye on her."

"Aye aye captain." I shake my head at Abby as I listen to three sets of footsteps leading away from the kitchen. "Wonder what that was all about?" She asks after a moment of silence.

"No idea." I tell her, but I have this sudden overwhelming feeling that this day is not going to go as planned.

After the guys abruptly left, Abby and I quickly finished breakfast and got ready to head to Doc's. The guys had an additional four men follow us in a separate vehicle. So me, Abby, Ares and two guards in the SUV and four others in a second SUV driving behind us. I think it's a bit of overkill, but I appreciate the sentiment.

It doesn't take long to get to Doc's office. I'm barely stepping my foot through the front door before I'm being led back to a room. The guards went to follow me, but Abby put a stop to that real quick.

"I'm pretty sure if the boss man found out you saw her naked, they might cut out your eyes." I'm pretty sure she thought it was a joke to say that but I think Jax might actually do it and the guys must have thought so too because they waited just outside the exam room instead.

The nurse has me change into a grown before collecting blood and urine, then checks me, my temperature, blood pressure and all that routine stuff nurses prepare for. It feels like an hour of wait before Doc knocks. "It's me, Miss Wren."

"Come in." I call, fidgeting with nerves now that Doc is actually going to examine me.

"Sorry it took so long, Dear. I had a few tests run before I came in. Xander told me a few of your symptoms, and I had a hunch." I'm not sure if that makes me feel better or worse. "But before we get to that, how have you been, sweetheart? I see you've made a new friend."

"Hi, I'm Abby, Wren's personal assistant, and this is Ares, her other personal assistant." I giggle at Abby's definition of Ares and herself.

"Yes, well, they sort of found me. How have you been, Doc? I haven't seen you in a while. Which, I suppose, is a good thing." I tell him, but he lets out a nervous chuckle.

"Well, I've been good and yes, it has been a while, but I suppose I'll be seeing you more often now." I frown at that. Why would he need to see me more often unless something is wrong? Xander was right. Something is seriously wrong. "Wren, you're pregnant."

Chapter Eighteen

Xander

I hate leaving Wren, especially now when she needs us. I'm glad she finally agreed to go see a doctor, and we trust Doc to take care of our girl. It helps that Jax called in an extra four men for protection duty.

I thought it was odd that all our phones rang at the same time, but it makes sense. Adrian planned this attack well. Three of our properties are on fire and each site has a report of seeing Adrian himself. My first thought was to split up to divide and conquer, but I have a gut feeling this is what Adrian wants. To take us out one by one.

With that in mind, we all hop into one SUV and head to the first location closest to us. It's one of our smaller warehouses that we keep back stock in. Pulling up to the drive, the entire place is engulfed in flames. They're so bright they make the morning light look dull. The fire department is already on scene as they work around the blaze. We watch for a bit from the car until we see one of our men standing off to the side.

Stepping out, we head straight to him. When he spots us, he takes a small step back in fear before holding his position like a smart man. "Boss." He greets.

"What happened?" I don't bother with pleasantries. I can see he's alive and well, a few scraps but breathing.

"It was a normal morning. Me and the others were doing our walk around when one of the men went radio silent. I headed for his position and found him dead. Shot. Seconds later, there was an explosion, then the warehouse went up in flames. It was chaos after. I heard more gunshots and when I rounded the corner of the building, I saw the man you've been looking for, Adrian, with at least three other men." Clenching my fist, I force myself not to react. Our men need to think we have this under control, so I give him a nod before turning on my heel.

"Stay on site until everything settles. Keep us posted." Jax gives him instructions before following me and Maverick back to the car.

We head to the next location and within seconds of being in the SUV, Maverick asks what I've been thinking. "This doesn't make sense. What's Adrian's game plan?"

"Better question, who does he have working for him that knows of these locations?" Jax asks. Which is also a good question.

"I don't know, but something doesn't feel right about all this. Strap up and keep your eyes focused." The rest of the ride to the second location is quiet. All of us processing what's going down and trying to anticipate Adrian's next move.

It takes about ten minutes to get to this location. It's closer to the edge of the city, but not as far as the last warehouse. This one was more of a meeting spot. When doing deals with out-of-towners, this was the spot we would meet at. It was a neutral ground between the city and highway out of town, with multiple escape routes in case anything went array. Pulling up to this warehouse, we can feel the heat wanting to caress us through the car. The fire department hasn't made it this far yet. Between last night's fires at Adrian's properties and now ours, they must be working overtime and running on fumes.

This warehouse is larger, built on a large dirt lot. The entire building is burning hot as we exit the vehicle and attempt to get closer. We keep our eyes open for any of our men, but after circling the building twice, there is no sign of our men.

Picking up my phone, I dial the man who was supposed to be on shift this morning. It rings a few times before Maverick jerks his head towards the tree line. He nods, pulling his gun from his waistband and making his way over. The sound of a phone going off gets louder as we get closer. Rounding the first tree where the sound is coming from, our guns raised, we see exactly why our men weren't answering. All three men who were stationed here are dead. Bullet holes riddle their bodies. This was an execution.

"Let's go. Mav, have men come collect them. We need to move; Adrian has an endgame, and we need to figure out what it is." My mind is flying through scenario after scenario as I head back to the SUV. The scent of burning metal fills my nose and my rage. We expected retaliation, but we didn't think he would move so quickly.

Mav makes the call as we all get back into the SUV and head for the last and furthest warehouse. This one is on the outskirts of the city and only accessible by a long dirt road. It takes us about twenty minutes to get here. On the way, Jax checks in with our men, letting us know Wren made it to Doc's and is seeing him now. They also clarified that only Abby went into the room with her, which is good because I'm sure Jax would scoop out a few eyeballs if anyone saw Wren naked but us.

Pulling up to the last warehouse, I slow our approach. I expected to see flames burning bright, more of our men dead with bullet holes, and our warehouse in shambles, but I don't see any of that. This building is untouched, but none of our men are in sight. Something from the corner of my eye catches my attention in the tree line a second before I hear the shot.

"Ambush!" I shout as I slam my foot on the gas. We shoot forward as bullets start to ting off the SUV, but don't get very far as at least two tires get shot out. Most of our vehicles are bulletproof, but they can only withstand so much until the metal gives. "Fuck. They are surrounding us."

"It's not going to hold!" Jax shouts from the back, currently crouched down like the rest of us. "We need to move."

"Wait for the reload." Mav calls.

I watch as Jax pops his head up a few times. "I'm counting seven, maybe eight men. They are slowly creeping in, so our best chance is going to be to head for the tree line over there." He points to the west. "There are two men positioned there. I'll take our tails." He reaches underneath his seat and tosses extra magazines to us. We all pull out our weapons before glancing around.

"We better all make it, or Wren is gonna be pissed." Mav says with a chuckle before switching gears and focusing.

"On three." I wait for the rain of shots to pause before giving my brothers a nod. "One." Deep breath. "Two." I picture Wren. "Three. Move!" Doors get thrown open in all directions as Mav makes his way around the front. We all move as one, a solid triangle, our back to each other as we return fire. I spot the two guys Jax mentioned and take them out quickly. I have no idea if Mav or Jax have hit any targets, but we don't stop until we hit the tree line.

The moment we take cover, we can hear tires on the gravel road leading to our position. Peeking around the tree, I spot additional men climbing out of a blacked-out Range Rover, but it's not our men. "Fuck, four more men just pulled up."

"We need to split up. Take them out one by one. This is our territory; we know it better." Jax is right. Checking our ammo, we make a plan to split and move around the property. The fire fight has paused, with each side weighing our options on how to move forward.

"Ready?" I ask, getting in position to move. We barely nod to each other in agreement when there is a huge explosion. The blast wave sends heat and metal flying right at us as we are thrown back. My ears ring as I get my bearings while trying to focus on where Jax and Mav landed.

Suddenly, a searing pain shoots through my shoulder as a bullet hits me. I'm pulled to the ground as Jax returns fire and Mav slaps me across the face.

"Get it together, Xander. We have to move. Now!" It takes my brain a second to register the fire fight has started again. The pain in my shoulder fades as I get my head back into the game. I stumble to my feet as we take off, using the trees as cover as we return fire. The warehouse is now up in flames but that's the least of my worries as I spot men dressed in all black moving around the lot aiming for us.

Once all three of us are in position, Jax gives the signal. It's now or never. The only thought I have as I round the tree, covering me from sight is I need to get to Wren. She's in danger. I can feel it.

That's when all hell breaks loose.

Chapter Nineteen

Wren

"Wren, you're pregnant."

I hear the words but at the same time I don't. I'm. Pregnant. I'm having a baby. I have a baby in my stomach. So, all this throwing up lately is morning sickness. I'm pregnant. Who knew three simple words could completely change my life?

I'm still sitting on the exam table, wearing a patient gown, when I feel Ares lean against my legs. I wiggle my toes against his warm body, hoping he somehow grounds me as I spiral.

Did I want kids one day? Of course. I love kids.

Was I ready to have a kid now? NO! Not with Adrian still being a threat and on the loose.

The guys and I haven't even had that conversation yet. It's not like we were being safe during sex, but I thought I was still covered by my last birth control shot. What if they get mad? What if none of them even wanted kids? What if, when they find out who the father is, the other two will want nothing to do with me? Oh god, I can't breathe. I feel like my lungs aren't working anymore. This can't be happening; Doc must be wrong. I can't be pregnant. My hands move to my flat stomach as worry floods my system. I'm pretty sure I'm hyperventilating now as my mind goes down a rabbit hole.

Will I even be a good mother? I won't be like other mothers; I won't ever be able to see my child. I won't be able to watch them run around and play. Not only that, but I won't get to watch a dance recital or a football game. I won't be able to tell if they have mine or their father's eyes. I'm going to be a terrible mother. I can't do this.

"Wren? Wren! Wren damn it!" I feel my body being jerked as Abby gives me a shake by my shoulders. When I focus on the here and now, I realize my face is wet. I'm crying. Arms wrap around me in a tight and firm hug as I just let it all out. Abby lets me as, I'm pretty sure, I've soaked her shirt with all my tears. "Talk to me. What's going through your head? Aren't you excited?" I shake my head no before nodding yes, then shaking my head again.

"Abby, I have no idea. I always wanted to be a mother; I love kids, but after I lost my sight, I didn't think I could. I mean, I know I can, but I didn't think I wanted to anymore. I'll never get to experience motherhood like other mothers. And what if the guys don't want a kid?" Abby lets out an audible snort at that. "What? It's true. We haven't talked about it, but what guy, let alone three, wants to be told one of them might be a father two months into a relationship. That's insane. What if they think I did it on purpose? That I'm trying to trap one of them." Another snort.

"Oh Sweetheart. I know you're blind, but I can see and the way those guys look at you are men obsessed. You practically hung the moon and stars to them. There could be a hundred beautiful supermodel type women in a room, and they would only have eyes for you." She lets out a giggle. "I bet you that super cute Coach purse I just got you last week, that the moment you tell them, they are going to be excited." I shake my head at that because it's so hard to believe, but Abby sounds so sure of it.

"Miss Wren, I know this probably isn't the best timing in the world, but I think your friend is right. Those boys have been so protective of you since the day I met you. It might not have been the best of terms, but I think you love them back now." Doc places his hand on my shoulder, squeezing just a bit to show support. "Would you like to hear the little heartbeat and maybe get an image to show your men?" My heart skips a beat at the thought, but I slowly nod my head. I suppose it won't be 100% real until I have proof. "Okay. Go ahead and lie back for me while I grab what I need."

I do as he asks and lie back, my mind still racing, but not in crazy directions anymore. No, now, my mind is going over everything I could possibly need for a child. Doctor's appointments I might need, vitamins I need to take, foods I should be eating or avoiding. There is so much to think about, I'm starting to get a headache.

"Alright, let's listen to the heartbeat first. Go ahead and lift your gown." I raise the gown up to my breast and rest my hands on top of it. I'm glad I kept on my underwear. "This is going to feel cold." A splash of cold gel lands on my belly, making me jump. "Okay, let's see here." I feel the pressure of the device Doc is using as he moves around my stomach in search of a solid thumping. It takes a minute or two before I hear it. "There we go." Thump, thump, thump, thump, thump. Like the little flapping of hummingbird wings. "Well, I wasn't sure if I would be able to hear it this way, but since I can, I'm guessing you are roughly eight weeks along, dear. I'll run your blood work to be sure, but the heartbeat sounds good." I smile at that.

"But I think it will be too early for an image right now, so let's schedule an appointment for in a few weeks. Okay?" I nod, cleaning off my stomach and sitting up. "Alright, I'll write you a prescription for some nausea medication, but it's completely normal. I want you to start taking some prenatal vitamins every morning as well." All I can do is continue to nod as Doc continues to talk. The thumping of my baby's heartbeat is the only thing I can process.

"I will make sure everything gets taken care of, Doc." Abby tells him. They exchange a few more words as I quickly dress, still in a bit of a daze. I heard a heartbeat. I'm going to be growing a human being. The thump, thump of a heartbeat just made it so surreal. I come to at the sound of the door closing.

"So Wren, how are you feeling?" Abby sounds cautious, and I don't blame her. When I first heard the words, you're pregnant, I spiraled but now...

"I'm pregnant. I'm having a baby, Abby." I turn to her, giving her a huge smile as my hands drift back down to my flat tummy. I try to imagine myself all big and swollen, and it's hard not to laugh. "I'm going to look ridiculous once I gain weight. I'm going to look as if I swallowed a watermelon." Abby lets out her own laugh at my description.

"I bet that still won't stop the guys from rubbing up against you. I bet it will only get worse. They won't be able to keep their hands off you." I sigh at that. Abby might be right, if the news doesn't freak them out first.

"I think we should go home instead of the shop. This changes a lot, and I think the guys should know sooner rather than later." Abby agrees, as we gather our things and say a quick bye to Doc on the way out. Taking a deep breath of fresh air, we climb into the SUV and tell the driver to head home instead.

We're ten minutes into our ride home, and I've gone over a hundred and one ways to tell the guys the news. From putting buns in the oven and telling them to check it to yelling "surprise I'm pregnant" as they walk through the door. But nothing sounds right.

"So, have you thought about what you might want? A boy or a girl?" Abby's innocent question sends my mind whirling.

If it's a girl, I'll have to worry about when she gets older and her father killing a boyfriend or two if he doesn't like him or, worse, he breaks her heart. If it's a boy, I'll have to worry about him learning to kill before learning to do anything else. The guys and I will have to go over a lot of ground rules for raising a child together if they stick around. Not that I don't think they won't anymore, but I still have a small fear of them finding out the actual father and the others not wanting to be involved anymore.

I give Abby a shrug. "Honestly, I don't mind either, as long as they're healthy and happy."

"I get that. So will I be like an unofficial official auntie because I have so many outfit ideas, with little itty bitty shoes." I giggle at that.

"Absolutely. I need you; I'll even baptize you as Auntie Abby." She squeaks with excitement.

"I'm really glad we met Wren. As you know, I don't have any family, and just the couple of weeks working for you made me feel not so alone anymore. I have no idea how I will ever repay you, but I'll find a way." She reaches over to hug me when the screech of tires then metal scraping against metal sound behind us.

My heart skips a beat as Abby's grip tightens around, and I reach for Ares in my lap. "Ladies, hang on!" One man yells from the front. I scream when our SUV gets hit from behind, causing us to swerve all over the road. I grip Ares tighter as Abby yells. "Get us out of here."

What is going on? Was there a car accident, and we were just in the wrong place at the wrong time?

I'm proving wrong when we're rammed from behind again. "Fuck, I can't shake him. Shit. Hang on!" Another hit, but this one was from the side, causing our driver to lose control.

"Wren!" Abby screams as the SUV rolls. I don't know how many times we roll, but when we finally stop, we've turned upside down. My head is pounding as I try to shake away the sudden fog.

"Abby? Ares? Hello?" I hear a soft whine, then a low groan from next to me. "Abby?" I ask again. Once again, I can hear Ares whining from under me. I need to get down. I need to get us out of here. I can hear what sounds like gunshots just outside. Reality comes crashing back. Adrian.

"W-Wren? Are you okay?" Abby's okay. I hear a loud thump as she releases herself. "Hold on, let me get you down."

"Abby, we need to hurry. It's Adrian. I know it." I hear her curse before shuffling closer.

"Okay, this is going to hurt." I give her a nod and she releases my seatbelt. I drop like a brick, landing hard on my shoulder.

The gunshot sounds closer now, and I know if Abby is caught with me, he will torture her or, worse, kill her.

Swallowing the fear and pain I'm currently feeling, I tell Abby to run.

"Abby, I need you to run. Take Ares and run. Please." I beg, shifting the weight off my shoulder.

"What?! No! I'm not leaving you. We can run together." She begs back.

"Abby. Please. I need you to run and hide. The guys will come, and they need to know what happened and who took me. If he finds you, he will hurt you, and I can't lose you. Please run." Tears have started to fall. This will probably be the last time I will see my friend. They fall faster now, knowing I never got to tell the guys one of them was going to be a father. "Please Abby. If anything happens, I need you to tell them about the baby. That I was excited. Please run. Run now!"

"We will see each other again. I know it. I'm an auntie now." I hear her shuffle. "I'll keep Ares safe until you return, okay?" Her emotion matches mine as I hear a whine come from Ares.

"Keep her safe, Ares." I tell him, and in return, I get a low bark of what I'm hoping is agreement. "Go!" I scream. I hear them exit the SUV, but have no idea where they go after leaving. I'm just hoping they get to safety before...my thought is interrupted by a voice just outside my door.

"Let that one run. We came for the blonde bitch. Let's grab her and get the fuck out of here before the cops show up." The man speaking has a deep foreign accent that I can't place, but I don't have time to process anymore as the door is ripped open and hands grip my legs and yank. I'm tossed onto the ground and quickly try to rush away, but I'm kicked in the back.

My entire body hurts as I lay on the ground, knowing what's about to happen next. "That's her. Knock her out and let's go." The same voice speaks.

"Please. Please don't do this." I beg not that I think it will help any.

"Shut the fuck up, bitch. You're a payday, that's all." A second later, something hard slams across my head and I crumpled to the ground again. I can feel warm liquid rush down my face.

My mind goes fuzzy as I feel someone lift me and toss me over their shoulder. Abby and Ares had to be safe now.

My last thought before it goes dark is that my guys will come, and I need to fight for our child until then.

Chapter Twenty

Maverick

The explosion of the warehouse going up in flames rattled my entire body when the blast reached us from our position in the tree line. It threw us all unbalanced, with Jax recovering first. I followed suit, my head still pounding, when I notice Xander still struggling. Calling his name a few times gets me nowhere, which means his ears are probably ringing as much as mine right now. I notice blood leaking from a wound in Xander's shoulder, but push that worry to the back of my head. I feel only slightly bad when I slap him across the face to get his attention, but it was the only thing I could think of.

"Get it together, Xander. We have to move. Now." I give Jax a nod before tugging on Xander as we move along the tree line to get a better tactical position, shooting as we go.

Xander stops first and takes his spot behind a tree, giving me cover fire as I continue to move further down. Once I'm in position, I wait for the signal and hope I can hear it.

Moments later, a loud but uniquely Jax's whistle sounds among the fire fight. As one, we round our trees and focus on whoever is the closest to us. I take down two men before I'm hit in the leg. My right leg gives out, saving my life as another bullet goes flying past my head. Ducking, I roll until I can take cover by a large piece of debris, maybe a piece of the metal wall. Taking a second to catch my breath, I quickly reload before peeking out again.

Xander is taking cover behind a car that must have been flipped during the blast, while Jax continues to shoot away. Dodging bullets left and right. I'll be surprised if he makes it out with only one new hole. From the corner of my eye, I see movement coming up behind Xander. A man dressed in all back, slowly creeping up. I move then, rounding the edge, gun raised, I take aim. I send three bullets soaring his way, and they all hit their mark center mass. Xander snaps his body around, gun raised, but lowers it once we make eye contact. Glancing down at the man now bleeding out on the floor, he gives me a nod of thanks.

We don't waste anymore, time jumping back into the fight. Send out bullets and dodging them in return. We underestimate the number of men who were originally here, and soon I'm dropping my weapons and picking some up from whichever dead man is the closest. It feels like hours before the sound of the firefight dies down, but I know it takes half that time. This was a planned ambush, and I'll have to thank Xander later for making the call for us to stay together. If it was only one of us, that one would have been dead. Adrian didn't come to play today, but he got too cocky, thinking we wouldn't be able to handle twenty plus men in a fight.

Jax and Xander check for IDs and phones, secretly hoping Adrian might be among one of the dead, but of course, he's not. He sent hired guns to fight his battles. That pussy. While they go off to do that, I look for a reliable set of wheels. Our vehicle was parked decently close when the bomb in the warehouse went off, leaving our SUV a little more than scrap metal at this point. The other vehicles I've spotted have been pretty shot up as well, but I'm hoping I can get at least one running enough to get our asses back to the city.

It takes me about thirty minutes of Frankensteining the last car that pulled up to run. It's not a high-speed chase type vehicle, but I think it will get us far enough to get to one. "Ready when you are." I call out as Jax and Xander toss the last dead body into the still burning building. We don't need any more bodies tied to us at the moment. Both men climb into the car, and we head back to the city.

"Jax, get a hold of our men with Wren. I want her home and the house on lockdown. Adrian wasn't at any of the warehouses, which means this was some type of diversion." Xander calls out, rotating his shoulder to get a feel for the damage in the backseat while Jax pulls out his phone and makes the call.

"Edward didn't answer." He hangs up before dialing a new number. That sinking feeling that something is wrong hits my gut and I slam my foot down on the gas. The car shoots us forward, and I pray it makes it back to the city before blowing up or something. "Still no answer." From the corner of my eye, I see him frown before dialing another number. "Wren's not answering either."

"Try Abby. She always has her phone in her hand." I say as I swerve around another car. We hit the city limits a lot faster than expected, and I head straight for our closest safe house. Pulling up, I barely have time to park before the doors get thrown open, and we are heading for the garage. None of us even bother to grab a first aid kit as Xander grabs the keys off the wall and opens the garage sliding door. Minutes later, we are back on the road.

"No answer on Abby's phone, either. I'm calling Doc." Jax says before calling the Doc. His phone automatically connects to the new car, and Doc's low voice fills the car stereo.

"Gentlemen, are you needing a house call?" he asks.

"Where's Wren?" Xander demands.

"Excuse me, Wren?" he asks.

"Where is she, Doc?" There's a rustling over the phone before the old man answers.

"She said she was heading home about an hour ago. Is everything okay?" he asks, sounding concerned.

"I don't know yet, but get to the house. We need some patch work done." Jax responds before hanging up and trying Wren again.

"I thought she was going to the shop after Docs. Why would she have been going home instead?" I ask, but don't expect an answer as Xander changes course to home.

We're about ten minutes from the house, worry causing all of us to be on edge since we haven't heard back from a single person. Wren's phone is off, Abby's and our men just keep ringing until it goes to voicemail. Not a single phone being answered. I keep my eyes peeled for anything out of the ordinary when I spot something off the side of the road. I squint as we get closer, a black blob down an incline off the side of the road. When we are close enough, I see two blobs. Fuck. No, no, no, no, please don't be what I think it is.

"Stop." I yell, causing Xander to slam on the brakes hard. We all going flying forward in our seats but I don't have time to care as I jet out of the backseat. Jax and Xander shout after me, but my adrenaline is pumping as fear rushing my body. "Please don't be it. Please don't be it." I chant as I side down the embankment and start running to what is clearly two rammed and smashed SUV. Two SUVs that look like ours. I'm halfway to the upturned vehicles when I see the first of our men. A clean kill shot right through his head.

"Angel!" I call as I hear the others following. "Angel! Answer me Baby."

"Princess!"

"Little bird!"

"Wren!"

I take the first SUV that's flipped upside down. I see another two of our guys and a few drag marks as I crouch down to duck in. Blood and broken glass are scattered all over the back seat, but it's Wren's purse that I spot next.

The contents spill about the now floor. "Fuckkkkkk. That fucker has her!" I scream.

"She might have gotten out. Where's Abby and the mutt? That dog wouldn't have left her?" Xander exclaims. He has a point. I take a second to survey what would have been their best options before letting out a loud, long whistle.

"Aressss!" I call and, as if he was waiting for his own signal, the damn dog barks. The three of us rush in that direction, following the noise before the dog himself rounds a tree. "Ares, where's Wren?" I ask and he jets off to the left. I give chase until I see a pair of women's tennis shoes a few meters away. Bending, I see that it's an unconscious Abby, bleeding from a minor cut on her head.

"I found Abby." I tell the other before scooping her up in my arms. "Abby? Abby? What happened? Where's Wren?" I'm panicking now because I don't want to accept that Adrian took her. The things he will do to her, to punish her for what his dark and twisted mind thinks she did wrong. Abby lets out a low, pain filled groan before her body goes limp.

"Wren's not here. He has her. Let's get Abby back and see what she can tell us. Doc is on his way." Xander says, leaning down to give Ares a pat on the head. What I would have done to get a picture of Xander Ashford giving a dog affection? Ares seems to be managing, but has a small limp as he walks along with me, as if still wanting to protect Abby. I have a feeling this is Wren's doing, since I know Ares wouldn't have left Wren unless ordered. He only ever listens to her commands. She might have saved both their lives by sending them away. Adrian is not a kind man and would have used Abby and even Ares against her if he could.

We make our way back to the car and climb into the back with Abby still in my lap. Ares jumps in after me and lies on the floor, a small whine in the back of his throat as he stares up at me. I know, little guy; I miss her too, but we'll get her back.

Xander slams his foot on the gas, sending us flying back, before he snarls at us. "Get every last one of our men to the house within the hour. If Adrian wants a war, he's going to get one."

For Wren, we'll all go to war.

Doc is already at the house and in our makeshift infirmary as we pull up. I head straight for the medical room with

Abby, Ares still attached to my side. Doc frowns as we enter, glancing behind me as if looking for someone else, someone like Wren.

"Where's miss Wren?" he asks, grabbing a pair of gloves from the counter.

"Focus on Abby, we need to know what happened?" He gives me a quick nod before nodding to the table. "Lay her down. What happened?"

"They were rammed off the road. I think they flipped a few times. Abby was found in the tree line unconscious." I set Abby on the table and Doc gets to work. Shining light into her eyes, turning her head from side to side. He takes a long look at the gash on her head before heading to the counter and grabbing a white pouch.

"I'm going to activate some smelling salts. This will wake her. It doesn't appear to have any major injury but she might have a concussion, but she should be able to tell us what happened." I give a nod to continue as Jax and Xander walk into the room. We all stand to the side and watch as Doc snaps the pouch, shakes it, then places it under Abby's nose. Like a shot of adrenaline to the bloodstream, Abby shoots up with a scream.

I rush forward to calm her. "Abby. Abby. You're safe. You're home." At the sound of my voice, her head snaps around the room.

"Wren? Where's Wren?" She climbs off the table. "We need to find her." She stumbles forward, and like she had just been struck by lightning, she stands at attention, a look of horror on her face as she turns to Doc. "The baby!" she exclaims.

The baby? What baby? A Baby?

Abby's and Doc's faces drain of all color as they turn to the three of us standing there, confused. "What baby?" Jax asks first.

Abby's eyes fill with tears as she opens her mouth, then closes it. Doc looks down at the floor before adjusting his glasses and sighing. "You weren't supposed to find out this way, but I feel this might burn that rage you have hotter." This time he looks up, making eye contact with each of us before dropping a bigger bomb than the warehouse explosion in our lap. "Wren doesn't have a stomach bug. She's pregnant. From my exam, we estimated she's about eight weeks along."

Pregnant. Wrens pregnant. With a child. A child who is ours. My brain can't process what is being said right now.

"How sure are you, Doc?" Xander asks, but there's an odd note in his voice. Doc pulls out a phone and pulls up a recording before handing it over.

"I forgot to send this to Wren earlier, so she had something to listen to or show you." Xander hits play and the sound of quick thumping sounds. I frown at the phone as Jax snatches the device out of Xander's hand and puts it to his ear, pushing play again.

"Is that...is that a heartbeat?" The awe in Jax's tone is clear as he hits the play button again and again. Doc just nods while I stand there like an idiot, still trying to understand that Wren, our Wren, is pregnant.

I would be lying if I said I haven't thought about getting her pregnant before. The guys and I have even mentioned how beautiful Wren would be as a mother to our children. We already knew she would be the only woman we would accept to have our children, but we also wanted to give her the choice. We've wanted to have this conservation for a while, but everything else just kept happening, so it wasn't the right time. Does Wren even want kids? It wasn't like any of us were using protection, but she knew that. Everyone knows sex equals a baby, so that means Wren might have wanted one, too.

Abby interrupts my thoughts. "We were on the way home, talking about a way to announce it to you all, when we heard a crash from behind. I tried to protect her. I tried to shield her, but someone hit us from the side, and we swerved off the road and flipped." She takes a deep breath, wiping away the water building along her lashes. "When we finally stopped, we were upside-down. I got her down, but I think her shoulder was injured. Then we heard the gunfire. Wren was yelling at me to run. I didn't want to leave her, but she told me you guys would come. She said it was Adrian. Oh, god. Why did I leave her?" Abby loses the fight with her tears as Doc wraps his arms around her in support. "She told me I needed to keep Ares safe and to tell you she loves you." The dog in question presses against her legs as well.

Out of nowhere, our fierce, usually calm, unofficial leader loses his shit. "I'm going to fucking kill him!" he yells before turning and punching the wall. "I want every single person who works for us on the streets. I want to know where that bastard is now. Offer an award for anyone who has information on his whereabouts, and if anything happens to Wren or that child, I will burn down this entire fucking city as payment for what I lost!" Another punch against the wall and he storms out.

"I'm taking the phone, Doc." Is all Jax says before he too storms out, with a look on his face that would scare the grim reaper.

I watch as they go before turning and facing Doc and Abby. "Doc, we need you to stick around. We all need a bit of patching up, but we will need you with us when we find Wren." I glance down at Ares, the dog looking sad and depressed, with his owner gone as well. "Abby, keep an eye on Ares and help Doc if you can." She gives me a tiny nod before I to leave the room.

I feel lost, not used to being this empty feeling in my chest, as I head for my room to quickly shower and change. I have to remind myself that my angel is a fighter. She won't give up so easily, and I have a feeling Adrian isn't done with us either.

Chapter Twenty-One

Wren

Have you ever reached a point in your life where you think ending it all would be better than the alternative? Laying here on this dirty wet floor, head pounding, body aching, I'm thinking it might be a better option. I awoke not too long ago with my hands tied in front of me and my mouth taped shut. I was thrown on the floor like a piece of trash they think I am. Now I have to wait and see the fate I'll have.

I slowly roll to my back to get into a less painful position, but it doesn't help. There's a coldness to where I'm at, and I've pinpointed a leak in a pipe nearby for the reason of the wet floor. It smells musty and rotten where I'm at. My guess is some type of basement or maybe a garage? I can't hear anything but my own thoughts and the drip,

drip, drip of the leaking pipe. Shifting a bit more, I feel something hard on my left. Reaching over, I feel a cold rough brick texture, a wall. Pushing past the arch, I pull myself up into a sitting position and lean against the wall.

Taking a second to breathe through the pain, I grip a corner of the tape on my mouth and yank. I have to swallow the scream that wants to escape as the adhesive rips away my skin. Next, I bring my hands up, dragging around the rope until the knot is facing me. Forcing myself to move, I use my teeth to pull apart the knot. It takes me a few tries before I get it loose enough to yank my wrist apart and the rope gives. Rubbing at my wrists, I can feel the raw skin from how tight some asshole tied them.

Slowly, I slide my back against the wall and stand, wincing at each stab of pain I can feel in my head. I can feel the dry blood flaking against my forehead and face as I move, along with other parts of exposed skin. I must look like something out of a horror movie right now. Attempting to rotate my injured shoulder, I realize it's pretty useless. Minor movements send sparks of pain shooting up my arm, but once again I have to focus on pushing past my pain and instead find a way out of here, or maybe a weapon.

Keeping to the brick wall, I quietly shuffle my way down. I take small side steps, keeping my attention on making little to no noise, also listening for anything that might alert me to when someone is coming. I make it to a cross wall and move my back to it to continue on. Ten steps into this wall, my foot leading hits something hard. I jump but manage not to scream. Moving my good arm out, I kneel and touch whatever I just kicked. Using touch, I follow the shape up to a flat surface. My guess is some type of worktable.

Memories of the night I lost my sight come racing back. Being tied to a chair in the middle of a basement room. A worktable on the far side of the room was in front of me. A set of stairs behind me and a couple of small windows to the right of the stairs. I could hear the dripping of water coming from somewhere as well.

It hits me then. This place. I know this place. I've been here before. I lost everything here. Focusing, I recall the set-up again. The worktable had a bunch of shiny tools on it, but I couldn't see what from where I was seated. Assuming nothing has changed, and that Adrian has underestimated me and my lack of eyesight, I'm guessing there is something on the table I can use to defend myself.

Taking a deep breath, I release it before biting my lip and reaching forward. I pray I don't injure myself in the process as I slide my hands across the flat surface. I shuffle to the side, moving my body as I go, but find nothing. My heart and hope begin to sink when my pinky hits something cold. The biting of my lip helped my startled response, but I can now taste blood. Moving past that sense, I wrap my hand around what I touched. It's lightweight and feels kind of small, even in my hand. Running my finger across it, I yelp at the sting when I realize it's some type of small blade. Gripping it tight, I continue on.

Keep moving Wren. It's not just us we have to think about now. We have something to live for now.

Reminding myself of all that, I move to where I think I remember the windows. They seemed highish from my memory, but I was tied to a chair then. I can feel a small cool draft as I approach an area, giving me hope that I might have a chance to live, when a door opening sends icy dread through my veins. Throwing myself against the wall, I rush back to the last corner of the wall I felt. I'm a caged animal at this point, and my best defense will be my back against the wall. With the knife I found at the ready, I wait.

I'm not even a bit surprised when a certain voice calls down the stairs, but it sends terror through my soul all the same. "Oh Dolly. I'm home!" The wooden stairs creak as Adrian makes his way down. I hear a click of a light switch, not that it does me any good. He must get to a point where he sees I'm not where I was left, the rope and tape discarded on the floor. "Dolly?" He moves down the stairs faster until I know he sees me. The bastard chuckles. "Oh Dolly. What do you think you're doing?"

"My name's not Dolly!" I scream.

"Tsk, tsk, tsk. Now — now. All those lessons and you didn't learn a thing. You were doing so well until you ran away from me." I can hear him moving around as he speaks so casually, but I can't pinpoint him.

"I didn't run away. You tried to kill me! You thought I was dead and had one of your lackies throw me out like I was trash." I snarl. I've always thought Adrian had a marble loose, but no one is perfect. I thought we were in love, but I was so stupid then.

"Dolly, watch your tongue, or I'll need to take that, too." I feel the air shift and I strike out, knowing it's him. I must get him because he curses a second later, but I'm not fast enough to strike again because he returns the strike with one across my face, sending me flying back against the wall. My already pounding head intensifies as he wrenches the blade out of my hand and grabs my face, pinching my chin in a hard hold. He's pressing in against me and I almost gag at the feel of his hard dick settling against my leg. "That wasn't very nice, bitch." He steps back but tosses me back at the same time. I stumble, hitting the wall again, but this time crumpling to the floor. Instinctively, I wrap my arms around my stomach, afraid of a kick while I'm down. To him, it probably looks like I'm just curling in on myself.

"You know Dolly, your eyes were always my favorite part of you. Those big, round blue eyes were so doll-like. That's why I call you my Dolly. All those lessons were for you, you know. You should have been grateful. I made you into the perfect woman. I was going to make you my wife, but then you had to go and ruin it. Now look at you, back at the beginning. I'm going to have to teach you everything all over again." He slowly runs his fingers across my face, causing me to jerk back.

"I'd rather die than be your little pet again." I spit and it's true. He'll kill me at some point regardless once he finds out I'm with child.

"You know, it was so easy to take you from them." He snarls the word "them," like a curse. "I knew I could get them out of the house if I simply repaid their little favor from last night. It wasn't what I had originally planned, but I improvised. So, I set a few fires of my own, but I made sure the last one was set just right. Unfortunately, they're like little cockroaches and don't know how to die properly, so now we are moving to Plan B." I hear the rustling of fabric before he speaks again, this time closer. "Now smile for the camera, Dolly."

"What are you going to do?" I ask, fearing the worst likely outcomes. Of course, the asshole simply laughs before getting up.

"You'll find out soon enough. I need to make sure everything is in order, then we can start relearning our first lesson. Don't talk back." I hear the creak of the wooden steps as he ascends, then the click of the light getting shut off, followed by the door closing, then locking.

The moment I'm alone again I break, my silent cry followed by tears that come in waves as I curl tighter in on myself. The only thing that gives me a little hope is that Adrian said my men didn't know how to die, which means they were alive. I still have a chance because deep down I know my men will come for me and if they found Abby, they will know they have more to fight for as well. Our child.

Chapter Twenty-Two

Jaxon

After Xander left in a rage, I followed him out, Doc's phone still clutched in my hand. Abby's and Doc's words float around in my head as I make my way to my room. Once there, I kick the door shut and lock it. Ripping my shirt off over my head, I head for the bathroom. Glancing in the mirror, I realize I'm covered in more blood than I thought. I look like a serial killer who just went on a spree. I know some of the blood is mine from the few shots I took and some knife wounds from the one or two hand to hand I dealt with. The blood doesn't even bother me, but I still grab a towel, wet it in the sink and at least wipe off my face and chest. Once I'm done with that, I head to the closet to quickly change. I don't even pay attention to what I grab, just throwing on whatever I touch first.

Feeling halfway clean, I take a seat on the bed and stare at the phone, still in hand. Pregnant. I hit play again, turning up the volume and listen. The rapid rhythmic thumping causes my heart to skip a beat. Our woman is pregnant. I'm going to be a dad. We're going to be an actual family. I've never thought far enough into the future to comprehend having a family of my own.

Who the hell would be dumb enough to have my kid? I'm a monster. A killer. A man who uses his fist more than his words. I hit first and ask questions later. Grown men are afraid of me and women usually cower in my presence. And now I'm supposed to help raise a child and hope I don't give them nightmares. How am I supposed to be a father?

I hit play again. Thump, thump, thump, thump, thump. Again. Thump, thump, thump, thump, thump. Again. The always raging beast that lives in my chest so persistently calms the more the thumping plays. Thump, thump, thump, thump, thump. Again. The only other thing that has ever made me feel this way is Wren.

The thought of what that bastard could be doing to her has me clawing at my face. He already took her eyes. What more could he want? The sick fuck is obsessed with her, that's clear, but why? A part of me knows why Wren is perfect. Unlike any woman, I have ever met, but Adrian doesn't want to covet it. No, he wants to ruin it.

There's a pounding on my door before Mav yells. "Jax, get your ass downstairs now. Xander got a message." I'm up and out the door, trailing Mav as we rush down the stairs to Xander's home office. The door is already open, but the office is trashed. Xander's usual desk decor and papers are thrown across the floor, broken glass and whiskey litter the far corner. A leather chair has been overturned, and an entire bookshelf has been tossed to the ground. It looks like an F5 tornado tore through the room in a matter of minutes. I spot his phone on the desk but don't make a move into the room yet.

"Xander, what the fuck is going on? You said you got a message with information." Mav raises his hands in defense as he steps into the room. Smart man, show the raging beast you're not a threat. Xander just nods to the phone, and I take that as my cue to approach as well.

Mav turns on the phone and the screen lights up. My eyes take a second too long to focus on what I'm seeing. Wren. Wren curled into a ball on a dirty concrete floor covered in filth, grim and blood. I focus on the bright red contrast of the blood against the usually creamy pale skin she has.

"He says if we want to keep her alive, he wants to meet." Xander's eyes turn cold like death. "To negotiate the terms of his new ownership of the city's underground dealings."

"Just like that. We give him the city and Wren lives?" I snort. "He can have the city; I don't give a fuck, but Wren is ours. And we're not stupid enough to think this was all about claiming territory over the entire city, right?" I look between the men I call my brothers. "He's not just going to let us walk away. This supposed meeting is to get rid of us." I tell them. I should know, it's what I would do. Hold something over someone's head, get them to meet, then bam. No more problems, solved with a single bullet to the head.

"I know, but with Wren's condition." He starts, but I stop him there.

"Condition?" I snarl. "It's not a condition, Xander. She's pregnant. With our child. Our blood."

"I know Jax. I want Wren and our child back just as much as you, but we need to figure out what he has planned at this meeting first. An ambush? Another fucking bomb? If we want to get our woman back, we need to play this right and not end up dead."

"He has a point, Jax. I don't think charging in headfirst will fix this." Mav turns back to Xander. "What are you thinking, man?"

Xander takes a second to think it over. "I have a feeling he won't even be there. He has Wren right now. He's been so focused on her the last few weeks, she's his obsession. I don't think he will leave her right now." He's quiet for another long minute. "I think it will be another bomb. Fires have been going up around the city for the last two days. What's one more, right? The address he gave is on the south side, near the industry area. He knows we'll be suspicious of the area, so he won't have an army of men hidden. Maybe a few to watch and make sure we go in, and so they know when to set it off, but he knows we aren't stupid. So, here's the plan."

Over the next fifteen minutes, we review Xander's plan and weigh the pros and cons. We've already sent a few of our men to get into position on the outskirts of the area. Climbing into the SUV, I tuck Doc's phone into my pocket for safekeeping, not that it matters since I can still hear the thumping of a little heartbeat in the back of my head playing on repeat.

It doesn't take long to get to the south side, but we pull up short of the warehouse meeting spot. Xander messages our men, letting them know we are in position before we all get out ourselves. Splitting up, we all head to the areas where at least one man has been spotted. Moving between buildings, I find the ladder I was looking for and climb. The guy I'm after is the only one that was spotted high up. Which makes me think he needs the vantage point to see when it's time to blow it.

Just as I round another corner, I see whom I'm looking for. Quietly, I tuck my gun in the back of my waistband and creep up. I watch my foot placement to ensure I don't give away my approach, since we need this all to be quick and efficient. Time is ticking for Wren.

I'm about to make my move when the gravel under my foot shifts. The man kneeling in front of me whirls around, eyes widening. Yeah, a guy my size can be a ninja too. He must realize who I am because he dives to the side where I know his own gun sits, but it's the wrong move. His fingers barely graze the butt of the gun before my hands wrap around his leg, and I'm dragging him back. Twisting around, he kicks out. His foot lands against the back of my leg. The leg with the gunshot recently stitched up by Doc. My knee gives out for a half second, but it's enough for the man to jump up and land another kick to my stomach. Another wrong move. He must think he is some type of Flash as he turns and dives for his gun again, but I've decided I'm over playing this game.

Grabbing the knife attached to my belt, I fling it at the man's leg. It hits true to aim and gets embedded deep in his muscle. He falls to the ground with a howl of pain, giving me time to get up and kick away his gun. Deciding this asshole pissed me off, one too many times, I punch him straight in the face for good measure.

Glancing around the roof, I spot exactly what I was looking for. A black backpack sits off to the side and against the ledge. Taking a peek inside, I pull out a laptop and hold it up. "You've been a naughty boy, haven't you?" The man glares as he holds the blade steady in his thigh. His face is covered in blood as well, so I must've broken his nose. Oops.

Opening the laptop, I glare at the password protection screen. Somehow, I don't think this asshole is ready to cooperate with me yet. My phone going off makes me grin wickedly. "You're in trouble now." I say as I answer.

"Ready when you are." I say, glancing over the edge to see if I can spot anyone yet.

"We're headed up now." Xander replies before hanging up.

"So, you're the cleaning crew, huh? I don't think this is going to be a successful job." I let out a deep sigh. "You could make this easier on yourself. Give us what we need to know, and we'll let you walk away and pretend this never happened." I attempted to give him a sincere and honest look, but I'm pretty sure it didn't come out that way. Which is fine because he knows I'm lying, anyway. Footsteps on the gravel sound before Xander and Mav round the corner, and I give them a nod before focusing back on the asshole.

"Look." I start, then reach forward and quickly yank out the blade I left in his thigh. "See, a sign of good faith." I wipe the blood on the backpack at my feet before sheathing it away.

Xander steps forward with a menacing look. "Your boss took something very important of ours, and we want it back. If you don't give us the information we want, we will hunt down every single person you have ever cared for and kill them one by one. We will make it painful, and they will know it was because of you." The man audibly gulps before looking at his computer in my hands and then at my face. I give him my best twisted smile and nod excitedly, so he knows I'll enjoy it all.

"It was just a job. I'm supposed to blow the warehouse once you three went in. Then call him to confirm you three were dead. That's all." His eyes drift from one face to another, but I see the twitch in his eye. There's more.

"What else? Where is Adrian West hiding?" I growl, pulling out my blade to show him I will use it again.

The man tries to scoot away but doesn't get far with Maverick standing behind him. "Look, that's all. Blow the warehouse, call to confirm, and pick up the other half of my payment." His eyes go wide at the last part.

"Where?" Xander growls.

"The address is in my backpack, but if I don't call him, he is going to know you're not dead. He will send more people after you." I snort. He can try.

Digging through the backpack some more, I find a small slip of paper at the bottom, a single address written down. "Well, that's why we are going to blow the place, and then you're going to make the call. If you mess this up, I'll skin you alive just for fun."

"I'll make the call, and you'll let me go, right?" I glance up at the others, then nod. The man does the same, studying our faces before nodding back. Deep down, he has to know he isn't walking out of here alive, but I'll let him believe whatever he needs to, to get my hands around Adrian West's neck. Handing him his computer, I turn to watch the fireworks.

"Blow it."

Chapter Twenty-Three

Wren

I have no idea how long I laid here and cried, but I have nothing left at this point. Why haven't my men come for me yet? What does Adrian even want with me? I'm just an object to him, but I'm more of damaged goods. I shake my head, of all my useless thoughts. I need a plan to figure out how to survive, not just for me but for my child, because I can feel it in my soul that my men are coming for me. We just need to make it long enough for them to find me.

I recall the basement in my mind again. Worktable, stairs, windows. I was seated in a chair, which means they probably keep a chair down here. Maybe I can use that as a weapon. It's worth a shot. I push myself past the pain and slowly crawl across the dirty floor. This will be the fastest and most efficient way to scan the room. I scan my hands in arches with each step. Sweeping them out in hopes of feeling for the chair or anything else helpful.

I don't know when Adrian will be back to torment me, but I can't lose any more time than I already have. Moving in a straight line, I find nothing before hitting the far wall. Turning, I do it all again. Continuing this several times until I'm on my fifth pass and I finally feel something. I jerk my hand back on reflex.

The unknown is scary, but it gets scarier when your sight is gone. You can't see the danger when it's right in front of you.

Taking a deep breath, I reach forward again. My fingers graze something cold, but it's not a chair. I trace the shape of the object a few more inches before a scream lurches from my throat. A body. From my guess, a woman. I've been down here with someone this entire time.

"Hey. Are you okay?" I call out, but then I remember how cold she was. Taking another deep breath, I reach forward again. The moment my fingers touch bare skin, I have to force myself not to react. Slowly, I move my hand up, and I find a face before moving to her neck. I check for a pulse, but I already know there won't be one. A tear falls from the corner of my eye. This is going to be me.

LOVE IS BLIND

The door unlocking sends me scattering across the floor to the closest corner. Pinning my back to the wall, I wait.

"That's great news. Send me over the video. My guest would love to see it." Adrian lets out a deep laugh as the stairs creak from his weight. The click of the light sounds before more steps descend. "Well, she can't see it, but she can listen. I have to go, but I'll have your money ready when you get here." There's a long pause before he speaks to me.

"Dolly, no more hiding. We have something to celebrate, after all. Now, come sit down so I can share it with you." I hear him shuffling around before I hear a small thump like something being dropped.

I shake my head, not wanting to celebrate anything with him. I know how he celebrates; I have scars to prove it. So instead, I stall. "Who is she?" I point toward where I felt the body. Adrian lets out another sick laugh.

"Oh her. She was just a fling, baby. She meant nothing to me. Honestly, it was just a business transaction." I frown because he knows that's not what I asked. I want to know who she is. She must have someone who cares about her, who's looking for her. Then again, Adrian likes all the control and attention. His "woman" isn't supposed to have friends or even thoughts of her own.

"But who is she?" I ask again.

"It was a gift to you, Dolly. Tiffany wanted you out of the picture. Like I said, it was a business deal gone wrong. She wanted those men, and I wanted you. So, we worked together. Tiffany gave me information and every once in a while, when I was missing, you, she would let me fuck her senseless. But I thought of you the whole time, Dolly. Tiffany decided she wanted more, until I found her making plans to hurt you. I couldn't let her do that. You're mine Dolly." The dead woman is Tiffany, the guy's ex fuck buddy. She was with Adrian at the gala and I knew she was a bitch, but no one deserved what Adrian probably did to her. "Like I said, she's my gift to you, Dolly. To show you how much I love you. No one else is good enough for me."

"You're wrong. You need help Adrian." I plea, because he's talking crazy. Talking about love like hurting someone you supposedly love is okay. I thought that was love once upon a time, but I was wrong. I know what love is now.

"Shut up!" he screams before my arm is suddenly jerked up, my body following as he drags me to where he wants. He shoves me down into a chair and I have to force the flashbacks away. I've been in this position in this basement with this man and almost didn't survive. "Now. I have something I want you to listen to. This is my apology gift." Confusion fogs my brain. What is he talking about?

The next thing I know, I can hear an audio clip playing and a man talking. "The targets are entering the warehouse now. Three...two...one...boom." A loud blast makes me flinch as Adrian laughs again. The sound manic like. "I wish you could see this, Dolly. The moment the warehouse goes up with all three of them in it. We won't have to worry about them anymore."

"Them?" I ask, hoping, praying it's not who, I think.

"Of course, them. Those assholes that stole you. That tried to brainwash you, Dolly. Xander, Jaxon, and Maverick are finally gone." I shake my head. Tears I thought were long gone, forming.

No, no, he's lying. They can't be gone. They can't. No.

Adrian roughly pinches my chin and forces my head up. "Are you crying for them?" I stay quiet. "Answer me. Did you love them?" he snarls, jerking my head even further up to the point of pain.

"Of course, I love them. They weren't monsters like you." I scream. I should have expected what came next, but my heart was breaking. Who knew heartbreak like this hurt so much more than actual physical pain?

One moment I'm sitting in a chair, the next, I'm slapped so hard across the face, I'm landing on the floor again. I don't bother trying to get up or even fighting anymore. Without my men, what's the point? "Oh Dolly. I thought we could work this all out, but I think I was wrong. I think you're too far gone now. They ruined you." I can hear Adrian pacing back and forward. "This is all wrong. You ruined it. You ruined everything." He yells. "I just needed you to be my Dolly again. My perfect Dolly. You just needed to behave and give me an heir. That was all." And like a switch, it hits me.

This child is them. The last small piece I have of them. I have to fight for them or at least die trying, right?

It takes all the strength I have to turn in Adrian's direction and grin. "I will always love them and choose them over you, so go to hell." I rasp out. Adrian lets out an inhuman roar of fury before advancing. There is little to nothing I can do as he grabs my legs and drags me across the floor before kicking me in the back. I cry out in pain, but my only thought is of my unborn child. In the next second, Adrian is straddling me, his hands going to my throat and squeezing. I gasp for air, and claw at any part of Adrian I can reach, but it's no use. I'm not strong enough.

"You stupid fucking bitch." Spit flies into my face as he screams at me, but I can feel my body going numb. My mind is getting fuzzy, and I try to fight it. I give it everything I have, but it's a losing battle.

Sleep sounds really good right now. I just need to close my eyes and the pain will go away.

Faintly, I hear a loud crash coming from somewhere, but it's just my mind playing tricks on me. Finally closing my eyes, I tell my child, I'm sorry for not being strong enough.

Chapter Twenty-Four

Xander

Every action I've ever made has always been under my control. I made the tough calls and lived with the consequences. I even slept like the dead most nights, but the moment Wren St. James stumbled into my life, it's been a roller coaster. Watching her from afar was easy, I was still in control of my actions. That was until Jax called us one night to let us know he needed Doc at the house ASAP and that the woman we had all simply became obsessed with overnight was injured. I think it was then that I knew we were doomed. That this tiny slip of a woman would forever hold the keys to the castle and the monsters within. It might have taken some of us a bit longer to come to that realization, but it was clear that Wren was going to be our end game.

None of us ever thought we could love a woman, let alone all be in love with the same woman. We've tried many times to make relationships work, but in the end, it never worked. They asked too many questions that we didn't want to answer. Others were like Tiffany, who only wanted power and money. Wren wanted none of that. She just wanted to be seen and loved. Seen and loved, she is. It's impossible to not watch her. The woman with no sight, who still seems to see everything. She knows when we need her, when one of us just needs a tender, loving touch.

I've never been in control when it comes to Wren. My Little Bird might not know it, but she controls my heart, body and soul and currently there's someone out there that thinks he can take what doesn't belong to him. He thinks that my brothers and I are just annoying little crumbs to sweep under the rug, but he fucked with the wrong people.

We had to play this right and ensure Adrian West truly thinks we're dead. That we're no longer a threat to him. What's more proof than video, right? So, we record a few of our men entering the building as the man who was supposed to blow us up starts to count down out loud. He does it slowly to ensure our men can rush to the back door and get to safety. The moment he hits one, the bomb goes off, the heat wave reaching us even up here. Metal and more go flying through the air as the entire roof of the warehouse collapses in on itself. I stop recording and give the man instructions on what to say to Adrian next.

"If you want to walk out of here alive, don't fuck this up." The man nods before making the call.

He places it on speaker as it rings a few times. Adrian answers on the fourth ring. "Is it done?"

The man glances up at me and I nod to continue. "It's done. I made you a video." He baits, waiting for Adrian's reaction. The video is taken from so far. You would never be able to tell who the men entering the building really are. Just that three bodies entered, then the explosion.

"That's great news. Send me over the video. My guest would love to see it." Adrian lets out a deep laugh. I can hear shuffling on the other side of the line before he speaks again. "Well, she can't see it, but she can listen. I have to go, but I'll have your money ready when you get here."

"I'll be there in thirty." The line goes dead, and the man stares up at me. "There. It's done. You're officially dead. You have his address. I can go now, right?" he asks, taking a small step back. Giving him a small nod, I turn to leave. I can hear the audible sigh of relief, which only makes me grin as I grab my 9 mm from its holster, spin around, aim, and fire. His eyes widen in shock for a moment before his head flies back, then his body crumples over the edge. Tucking the gun away, I smirk.

"Shouldn't have fucked with the wrong men." I say before turning to Mav and Jax. "Now let's go get our woman."

The address on the piece of paper is only ten minutes away from the warehouse. Not wasting a minute, we head in that direction. Each of us is strapping on more firepower and ammo on the drive. We have no idea if this is Adrian's home base or if he has more men with him. Parking down the street, we slowly make our way up the drive. The house at this address is a large two story with a run-down feel. It's definitely seen better days, but it's also large enough that we may need time to search for Wren.

When we reach the side of the house, I turn to my brothers. "We go in quiet. No guns unless absolutely necessary." Turning back to the front, I pause, looking over my shoulder. "And I want Adrian alive." Two nods is all I need before we head in.

Like a well-oiled machine, we enter through the front and move as one to clear room by room. The entire house is quiet as we quickly split on the first floor. I head straight back, entering the kitchen before clearing the dining room next. Mav and Jax join me after a minute, each giving me a single shake of their head to let me know they found nothing as well. I point to the ceiling and move back down the hall to the stairs, letting them know we are headed to the second floor, when I hear a muffled noise coming from a door to my left. I pause, tap my ear, and point to the door. Jax nods before moving into position. Holding up three fingers, I count down. Three... I grip the knob... Two... I twist the handle slowly to make no sound... One... I yank open the door, allowing Jax to rush in. Mav and I follow suit as Jax heads down a set of stairs.

Jax's large body hides the view of what I now know is the basement, but halfway down the steps, his entire demeanor changes. That's when I hear Adrian.

"You stupid fucking bitch." Jax charges forward like a bull in a china shop before I can get a full view, but when I do, my body turns icy cold. There, on the floor, Wren lays lifeless, Adrian's hands wrapped around her tiny neck before Jax tackles the dead man to the floor. I stand there frozen in shock, or maybe disbelief, before Maverick shoves me to the side and rushes to Wren. He falls to his knees and shakes her.

"Wren! Angel, baby. Open your eyes. Come on Angel." I'm still standing there at the bottom of the wooden steps, just staring at the scene in front of me. Jax is slamming his fist into Adrian's body. Not a single inch going untouched. Maverick is hovering over Wren, checking for a pulse.

I'm losing control. I can feel the strings snapping. This can't be happening.

"Xander!" Mav yells at me, giving me some focus. "Get your ass over here, now." I move then, rushing to him and Wren, before checking her pulse myself. Fuck. She's not breathing. Without thinking, I start CPR. Interlocking my fingers, placing my palms on my Little Bird's chest, and start with compressions.

"Stop Jax. I want Adrian alive." I snap out. "And call Doc. Now!" he turns to do as I say as I stare down at our woman. Bruising has already formed around her neck in the shape of handprints. Glancing down at her body, I check for other injuries but find none that show with her still dressed. My eyes pause on her stomach. Our child is in there. "Come on, baby, breathe for me." I lean down, tilt her chin back, pinch her nose and give her two breaths before continuing compressions. "Come on, baby. We need you. We can't live without you, Wren." My brothers join me, all placing hands on her, needing to touch her, as I go in for another two breaths. My heart is physically breaking as I pull away to start another round of compression, but right as I place my hands to push, Wren jerks up with a raspy inhale.

"Wren!" we all shout but it's short-lived as she once again passes out, but this time still breathing. I scoop Wren up as gently as I can before heading to the stairs. "Knock him out and tie him up for now. Have our men come secure him. Wren needs a hospital now!" I call out.

Jax quickly delivers a solid punch to Adrian's face before quickly tying his hands. "I'll call Doc and have him meet us there." Mav calls from behind me as Jax catches up with us in the car. I climb into the back, careful of tussling Wren in my arms as Jax hops in the driver's seat and takes off. Mav makes the calls to Doc and our men from the passenger seat, constantly peeking back to look at Wren.

The drive to the hospital doesn't take long but is still not fast enough, but Doc is already there with an entire team of nurses ready to take over care. We've barely put the car into park when my door is ripped open and Doc is there. Stepping out, I place her on the gurney, momentarily afraid to release her. "Xander, let us take care of her."

"She wasn't breathing when we found her. I had to do CPR. Is the baby going to be okay?" I ask. Staring after Wren, as the other support staff wheel her away. Doc gives me a look that I can read loud and clear. It's too soon to tell. He seizes my shoulder, squeezing before following after Wren.

Maverick is to my left, holding back an emotional Jax, straining to get to Wren. "Enough!" I yell. "Get your shit together, Jax. Wren needs us here and if you're going to act a fool, they will kick us out. Doc is with her and will give us an update as soon as possible. Wren is breathing. She's safe now." The word safe coming from my tongue tastes like a lie. If she was safe with us, she wouldn't have been in this position in the first place.

Jax glares over at me before shaking out of Mav's grip and heading for the hospital's doors. Mav quickly follows, partly to ensure Jax doesn't cause destruction or murder anyone. I just stand there, the image of Wren's lifeless body laying on the floor burned into my brain and projected everywhere I look.

Little Bird, if you don't make it, I'm following you into the afterlife.

Chapter Twenty-Five

Wren

Waking up in an unfamiliar bed to the sound of loud, obnoxious beeping, the constant beep beep beep, not helping the pounding in my head. My entire body hurts as I take a mental inventory of my injuries. The pounding in my head making it hard to remember why I feel this way.

Think. Think. Think. What's the last thing I can remember?

I woke up, argued with Xander about going to the doctors. I had breakfast, banana chocolate chip pancakes, then the guys had to leave after getting phone calls, but I finally agreed to go see Doc. Like a flash of lightning going off in my mind, I see the entire day play out after that.

Doc telling me I'm pregnant, hearing the little thump of a heartbeat. I left with Abby, deciding to go home instead of work, but we were ambushed and ran off the road. I made Abby take Ares and run. Two men knocked me out and the next time I woke up, I was in Adrian's basement of horrors. Then he played that clip of an explosion. He said my men were dead. Oh, god. They're gone. Then Adrian snapped his hands around my neck. I couldn't breathe, I can't breathe.

I'm clawing at my neck. I need to breathe; I need to get his hands off me. I'm thrashing at this point, kicking, screaming, fighting for my life.

"Wren. Wren! Wake up! You're safe, Little Bird. You're safe now." I hear the deep timber of Xander but that's not possible. Adrian said he saw them die.

"Princess!" I hear Jax's voice next.

"Angel!" Maverick voice comes next, sounding panicked. "Shit. Doc!"

Everything is happening so fast. So many noises at once. I can feel hands touching me, only causing me to panic more. What is happening?! Where am I?!

A gentle and familiar, trusting voice speaks next to my ear. "Wren, dear. I need you to breathe and calm down, or I'm going to have to give you a sedative. You're safe dear.

You're in the hospital now." Doc explains as his words break through the hazy fog.

I'm safe. I'm at the hospital. Slowly, my breathing evens out and I focus on my senses. I can smell Xander's scent of whiskey mixed with cigars smoke. Jax's gunpowder and his favorite aftershave. Last, I can smell Maverick's fresh clean scent with a hint of fallen rain from his body wash. My men, they're here. They're alive.

I open my mouth to speak when raw pain shoots up the back of my throat. I'm thrown into a coughing fit before someone gently touches my face and places a straw at my lips. "Small sips, Princess." Jax says. I take a small sip like he warned, and the cool liquid instantly relieves the pain temporarily.

"Wren, dear, I'm going to need you to refrain from speaking for a few days. Your vocal cords were injured in your attack, so they need some time to heal." At the word attack, I stiffen. Attack is an understatement. Adrian tried to kill me and my child. My child. Oh god, I'm a horrible mother. How could I forget I was pregnant? My hands fly to my stomach in fear. Doc must understand my question as he rushes to continue. "Your baby is okay, sweetheart. I'll be monitoring you closely over the next few months, but their heartbeat still sounds healthy and strong." I sag in relief at that news and give him a small nod of thanks.

"Okay then. I'll let you get some rest. I'll come check on you soon." The closing of a door has me on edge again as I wait for someone to speak. I can feel their presence around me and it's overwhelming.

Mav speaks first. "Angel, we are so glad you are okay. We were so worried for a while but Doc ensures us you're going to heal up just fine."

Jax immediately jumps in next, giving me an even bigger sense of relief with his words. "Oh Princess. I'm so sorry you have to go through this, but you don't have to be afraid of Adrian ever again." He pauses, his tone changing slightly. "He is getting what he deserves." I don't bother attempting to speak. I can feel the damage when I just swallow, but I have so many questions.

What happened to Adrian?

Is he gone forever? As in dead?

What is he getting that he deserves?

These and so many more come to mind, but there will be another time for that. The room goes quiet again. The only sound is the beep of various machines before my last and final man speaks. I don't know what I was expecting, but it wasn't this at first.

"The Cozy Nook is being taken care of for the next month or so until you get the clear go ahead. I have made arrangements to get everything you need for recovery sent to and set up at the house. Abby is safe and taking care of Ares, who has seen a vet for an injured leg. It was a minor fracture, but he will be fine. Abby sustained a few bumps and bruises and a mild concussion, but Doc has already cleared her." Xander sounds so robotic, clinical, unlike the man I fell in love with. I knew he was cold and analytical at times, but this, this isn't my Xander. A tear escapes my lash faster than I can hold, but a rough thumb wipes it away. The bed dips before hands cup my face. "Fuck. I'm sorry, Little Bird. Please don't cry. I'm sorry. I- Fuck. I was so fucking worried. We thought we lost you. That we lost our child. We found you lifeless and thought you were gone. I didn't know what to do. I didn't know if I could live with you." More tears escape, but this time it's from something more. From the relief that I wasn't alone in that feeling of not being able to live without them.

Xander shifts position before I feel three hands run across my belly. "We're going to be dads, Wren, and you're going to be a mother. Since this wasn't the way any of us planned to find out. I speak for all of us when I say, you have made us the happiest men alive, and there's only one thing left to do. You're going to have to marry us."

It took the guys a couple of weeks to finally let me get back to a semi-normal routine. One of them is still always with me, but I honestly think it's to make themselves feel better more so than for my protection, like they still claim.

Last night, the guys finally told me something they've been keeping from me. At first, I was a little upset, but they gave me something to think about. This morning, I finally made my decision, and the nerves that are flooding my system right now are insane. I've been in the car with Mav for the last ten minutes as he takes us to where we need to go, and I absolutely want to puke right now.

"We don't have to do this if you don't want to." He says, but I shake my head. I need to do this.

"No. I can do this. As long as you all stay with me." I tell him as he reaches over and grips my head, giving it a firm squeeze.

"Always Angel."

The rest of the drive is quiet as I go over the last couple of months in my mind. From getting kidnapped to sleeping with my kidnappers. Meeting new friends and falling in love with not one but three men. I slide my free hand against my stomach. To fighting for something more than myself. It's for sure been a wild roller coaster ride, but from where I'm sitting, I think I would do it all again.

The car finally stops after a while and when I step out, I can feel rough, uneven ground. I can smell the wild fresh air, making me think we are in a forested area.

"Little Bird," Xander calls out from somewhere in front of me. I wait for Mav to reach my side, tuck my arm around his, he guides me to where we need to go. "You can turn back now." Xander says, leaning in to kiss my forehead.

"I've already told her that. She wants to do this," Mav replies for me. I give them both a firm nod as I straighten my back and take a deep breath.

"I'm ready."

My men guide me into a building where the temperature gets colder. It reminds me of a walk-in freezer, fancy restaurants have. The texture under my shoes changes to a smooth, hard concert. The smell is horrendous, causing me to wrinkle my nose in disgust. It's so bad, I don't want to breathe. "Breathe through your mouth. We won't be here long." Mav whispers in my ear. I do as he says, and it makes it easier. A few more steps, and we come to a stop.

"Princess. How are you feeling?" I send a gentle smile in the direction I heard Jax's voice.

"I'm okay. Just want this officially over." I tell him.

"Well, let's get started." There's a pause before I hear a muffled scream. "Wakie, wakie Adrian. I told you we had a special guest coming." Jax is in front of me in the next sec. "I wish you could see him as he is right now, baby. Unfortunately, he can't see or speak, but he can hear you." I place my hand on Jax's firm chest.

"Thank you, Big Guy." Jax grabs my hand and pulls me forward before moving me to stand in a certain spot.

"He is right in front of you." Cold metal is placed into my palm. "Are you sure about this? One of us can do this instead." I shake my head.

"No! I need this." My hand is raised until the point of the blade hits something firm. Adrian lets out another muffled scream, but I ignore it like he ignored mine all those times.

"It will be a killing blow when you're ready." Xander tells me from my right. I can feel all my men surrounding me, giving me the strength. When I told them what I wanted to do this morning, I could hear the hesitation to bring me, but I think they understood why I needed this as well.

Taking one last deep breath, I speak. "Thank you, Adrian. For breaking me. For leaving scars on my body. For teaching me what love wasn't. Because of you, I found strength. I found my scars don't affect me anymore. I found out what love really is. So, thank you, but I can't allow you to ever hurt me again. Goodbye." Without thinking, I use my body weight to push the blade in. There's resistance, but I push past it. The muffled screams don't stop, but neither do I. Tears have started to flow freely down my face, but I can't stop until it's done. Until I know Adrian West is gone, for good.

A hand on mine makes me jump before I'm turned into a firm chest. "It's done Wren. He's gone. You slayed your only demon."

My men lead me out of the building and the second I breathe in the fresh air, it's like I'm breathing for the first time. Because for once, I finally feel free.

There's a saying that love is blind. That when you're in love, you only see what you want, and it's true. But I'm no longer blinded by love because I can no longer see. I can only feel and these men, I once thought monsters, show me what love is every single day.

Sometimes love hurts, but this time, love heals.

Looking for a what happened next chapter?

Follow me on REAM for exclusive content, bonus scenes and so much more.

With three tiers to choose from and even follower benefits there is something for all my readers.

https://reamstories.com/nowensauthor

Acknowledgements

Huge shout out to my amazing girl gang! Melissa, Tabatha, and Natalie, you ladies were amazing! Thank you so freaking much for the support, and feedback!

STALK ME
I LIKE IT.

Also by N.Owens

Running from my past isn't easy. Always looking behind my back. I'm a freak. I didn't mean to hurt him, but he pushed me too far. It was self-defense, I swear. I just don't know what I did, so I ran and have been running ever since, until Ash Valley. Something told me I had to be here. Now that I am, my whole world is unraveling. These things shouldn't be possible but, here we are. And here they are. They call them the Chaos Kings.

Also by N.Owens

I was fine with the life I lived. After what happened, I settled into not being wanted by everyone. I'd become invisible, and I liked it that way. I had my Gran, a shitty job, and my love for photography. What else did a girl need? I'd planned to save enough to get me across the country, I just had to play my cards right.
Everything was in place until they showed up.
Beautiful bastards that forced their way through my carefully crafted walls. It took one night with all three and I knew I belonged to them. Dante, Chase, and August were all Heathens.

They woke up the part of me that I tried to keep hidden, making me realize that red looks really good on me.

My name is Dawn meaning first light but I'm the furthest to sunshine as possible. They don't see the real me, only the one I allow. They call me the good girl, the safe bet, vanilla at best but they have no idea what hides in the dark.
Until him.
He sees all the naughty, dark, depraved things I want. I should probably be more afraid, since he is my stalker and all but I crave the way, he secretly watches me. I imagine it's him in all my twisted desires, shadowed by darkest, whispering all the dirty things he wants to do to me.
We've been playing a cat and mouse game, even before he made himself known but I think it's time we start the real game of catch me if you can.

Also by N.Owens

I WON FAIR AND SQUARE, ATLEAST I THOUGHT SO.
LEXI-
The plan was simple. Walk in, settle my deadbeat dad's debt, walk out and finally wash my hands of my father once and for all. That was the plan at least. Until it goes all wrong and I'm left playing my cards right in a game of poker to win my freedom.

LUCKY-
I've always been lucky, that's how I got my nickname after all. But when Lexi walked in thinking she could just walk out after settling a debt she didn't owe, I knew I had to put my luck to the test. She thought she won but she was wrong. Because the moment I saw her I knew she would be the one.

Made in the USA
Middletown, DE
28 July 2024